Sweeties

charmz™

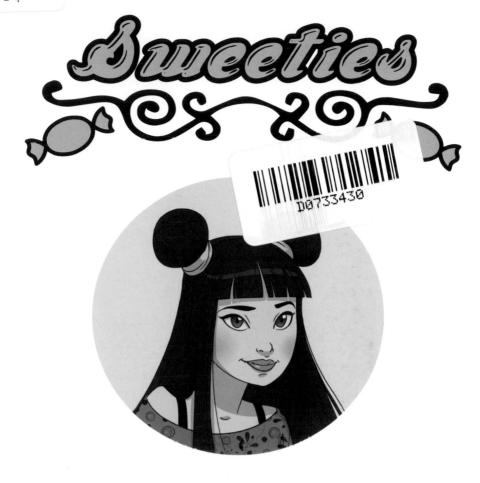

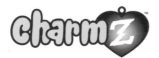

MORE GREAT GRAPHIC NOVEL SERIES FROM

charmZ

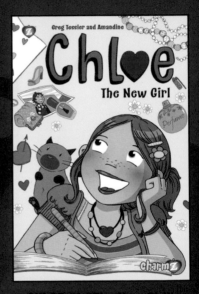

STITCHED #1 "The First Day of the Rest of Her Life"

CHLOE #1 "The New Girl"

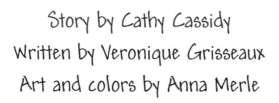

Story by Cathy Cassidy

Written by Veronique Grisseaux

Art and colors by Anna Merle

NEW YORK

Based on the novel "The Chocolate Box Girls-Cherry Crush and Marshmallow Skye,"
by Cathy Cassidy, first published by Puffin Books (The Penguin Group, London)
The Chocolate Box Girls Cherry Crush © 2010 by Cathy Cassidy
The Chocolate Box Girls Marshmallow Skye © 2011 by Cathy Cassidy
Comics originally published in French as *Les filles au chocolat* volume 1
"Cœur cerise" © Jungle! 2014 and *Les filles au chocolat* volume 2 *"Cœur guimauve"*
© Jungle! 2015 Jungle!, Miss Jungle! and the Jungle! logo are ® 2016 Steinkis Groupe
www.editions-jungle.com

SWEETIES #1
"Cherry/Skye"

Original story: CATHY CASSIDY
Comics adaptation: VERONIQUE GRISSEAUX
Cover artwork: ANNA MERLI & RAYMOND SÉBASTIEN
Interior comics art: ANNA MERLI & CLAUDIA and MARCO
FORCELLONI, YELLOW WHALE CREATIVE STUDIOS
JOE JOHNSON — Translation
SASHA KIMIATEK — Production Coordinator
JEFF WHITMAN — Assistant Managing Editor
MARIAH McCOURT — Editor
JIM SALICRUP
Editor-in-Chief

Charmz is an imprint of Papercutz.

HC ISBN: 978-1-62991-773-3
PB ISBN: 978-1-62991-764-1

Printed in China
May 2017

Charmz books may be purchased for business or promotional use.
For information on bulk purchases please contact Macmillan
Corporate and Premium Sales Department at
(800) 221-7945 x5442

Distributed by Macmillan
First Charmz Printing

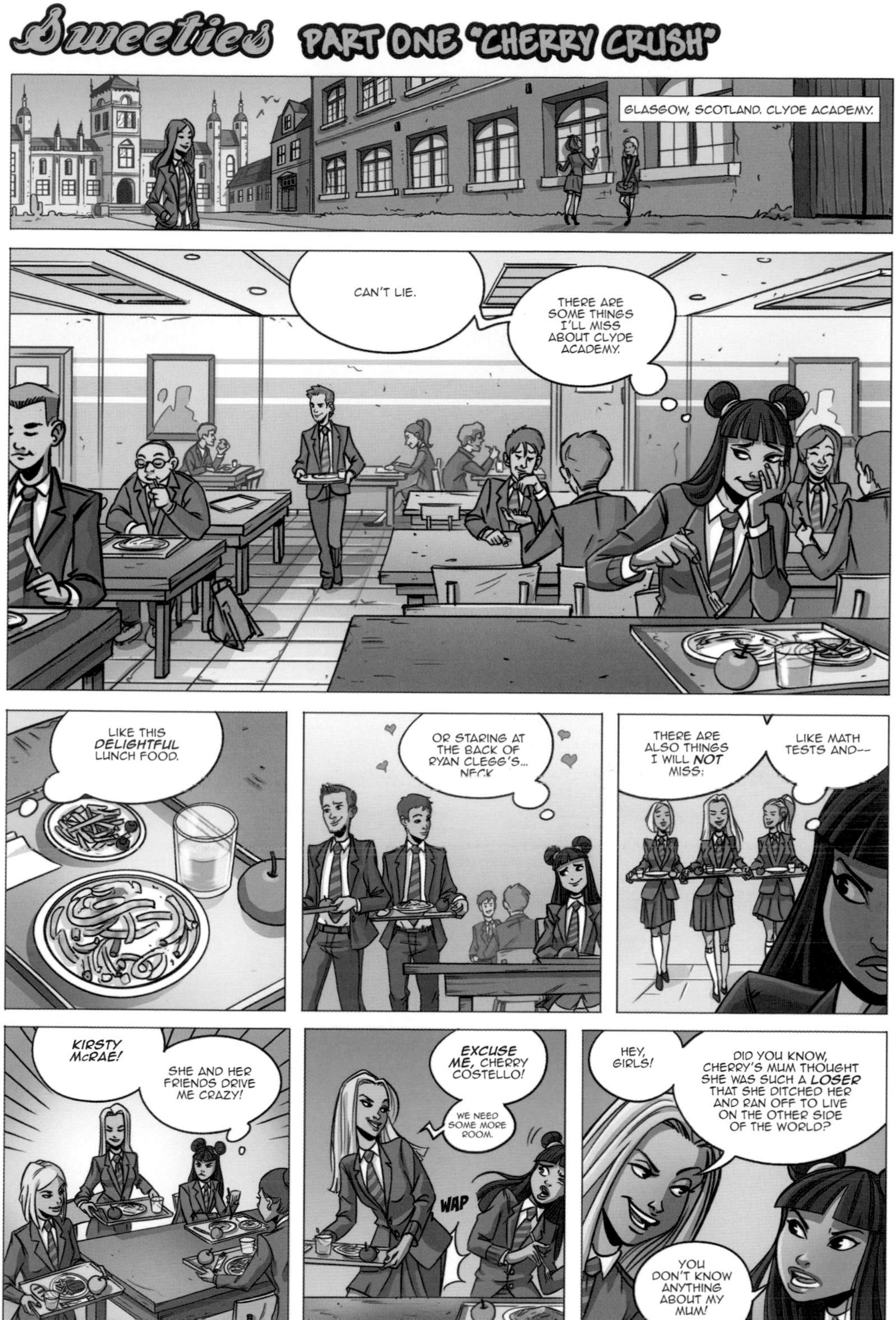
Sweeties PART ONE "CHERRY CRUSH"
GLASGOW, SCOTLAND. CLYDE ACADEMY.
CAN'T LIE.
THERE ARE SOME THINGS I'LL MISS ABOUT CLYDE ACADEMY.
LIKE THIS DELIGHTFUL LUNCH FOOD.
OR STARING AT THE BACK OF RYAN CLEGG'S... NECK.
THERE ARE ALSO THINGS I WILL NOT MISS:
LIKE MATH TESTS AND--
KIRSTY McRAE!
SHE AND HER FRIENDS DRIVE ME CRAZY!
EXCUSE ME, CHERRY COSTELLO!
WE NEED SOME MORE ROOM.
WAP
HEY, GIRLS!
DID YOU KNOW, CHERRY'S MUM THOUGHT SHE WAS SUCH A LOSER THAT SHE DITCHED HER AND RAN OFF TO LIVE ON THE OTHER SIDE OF THE WORLD?
YOU DON'T KNOW ANYTHING ABOUT MY MUM!

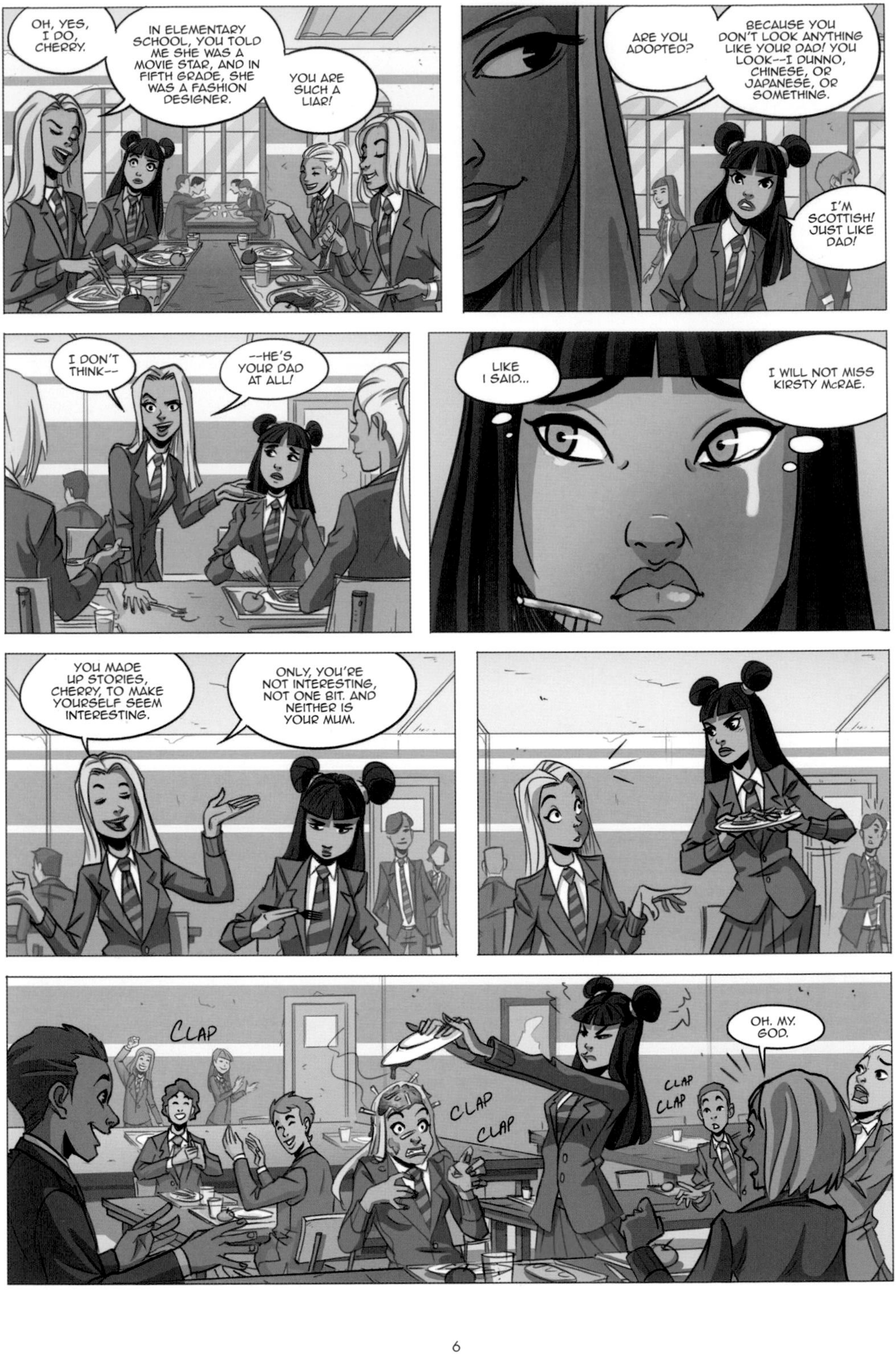
OH, YES, I DO, CHERRY.
IN ELEMENTARY SCHOOL, YOU TOLD ME SHE WAS A MOVIE STAR, AND IN FIFTH GRADE, SHE WAS A FASHION DESIGNER.
YOU ARE SUCH A LIAR!
ARE YOU ADOPTED?
BECAUSE YOU DON'T LOOK ANYTHING LIKE YOUR DAD! YOU LOOK--I DUNNO, CHINESE, OR JAPANESE, OR SOMETHING.
I'M SCOTTISH! JUST LIKE DAD!
I DON'T THINK--
--HE'S YOUR DAD AT ALL!
LIKE I SAID...
I WILL NOT MISS KIRSTY McRAE.
YOU MADE UP STORIES, CHERRY, TO MAKE YOURSELF SEEM INTERESTING.
ONLY, YOU'RE NOT INTERESTING, NOT ONE BIT. AND NEITHER IS YOUR MUM.
CLAP
CLAP
CLAP
CLAP
CLAP
OH. MY. GOD.

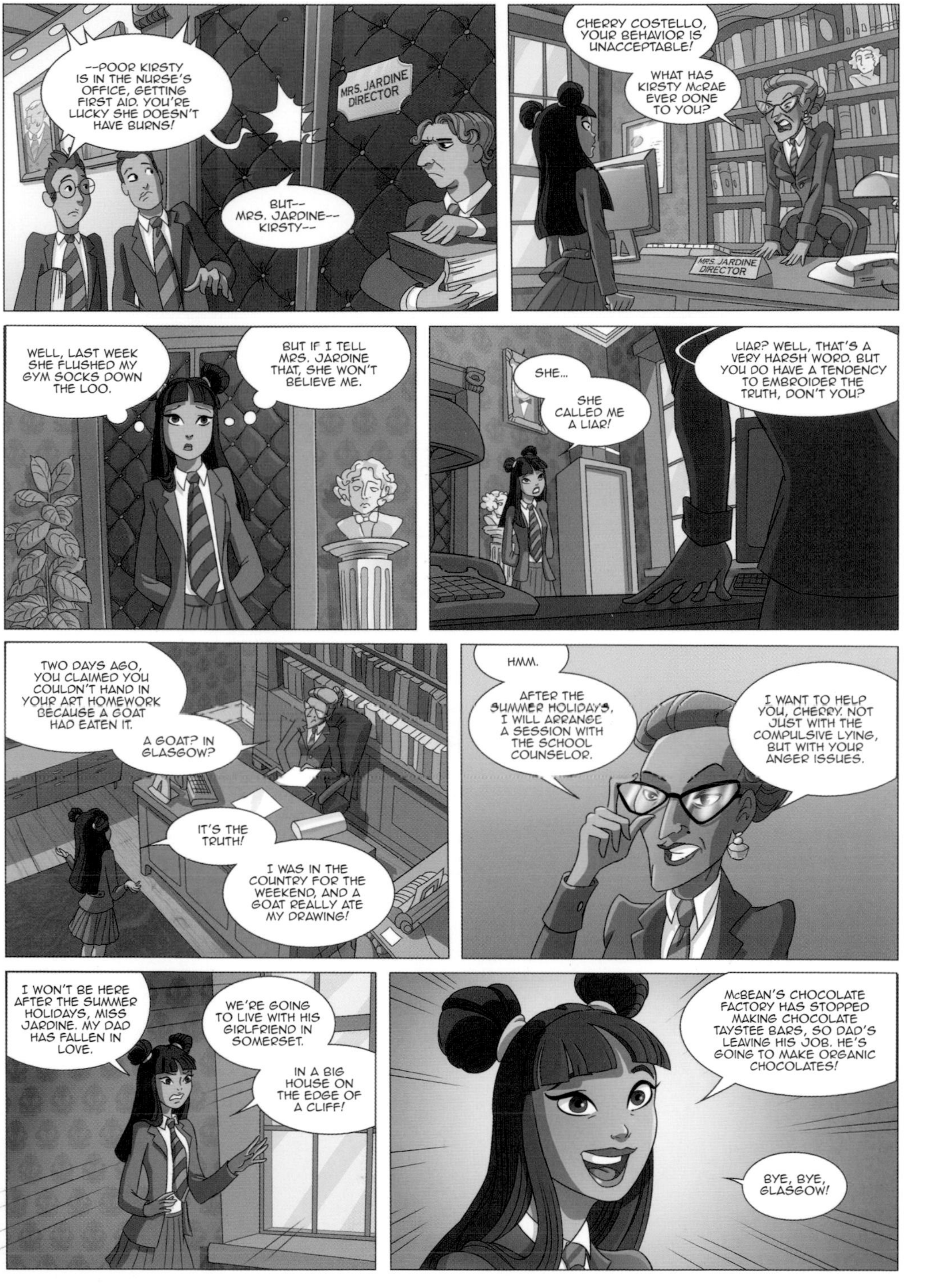
--POOR KIRSTY IS IN THE NURSE'S OFFICE, GETTING FIRST AID. YOU'RE LUCKY SHE DOESN'T HAVE BURNS!
MRS. JARDINE DIRECTOR
BUT-- MRS. JARDINE-- KIRSTY--
CHERRY COSTELLO, YOUR BEHAVIOR IS UNACCEPTABLE!
WHAT HAS KIRSTY McRAE EVER DONE TO YOU?
MRS. JARDINE DIRECTOR
WELL, LAST WEEK SHE FLUSHED MY GYM SOCKS DOWN THE LOO.
BUT IF I TELL MRS. JARDINE THAT, SHE WON'T BELIEVE ME.
SHE...
SHE CALLED ME A LIAR!
LIAR? WELL, THAT'S A VERY HARSH WORD. BUT YOU DO HAVE A TENDENCY TO EMBROIDER THE TRUTH, DON'T YOU?
TWO DAYS AGO, YOU CLAIMED YOU COULDN'T HAND IN YOUR ART HOMEWORK BECAUSE A GOAT HAD EATEN IT.
A GOAT? IN GLASGOW?
IT'S THE TRUTH!
I WAS IN THE COUNTRY FOR THE WEEKEND, AND A GOAT REALLY ATE MY DRAWING!
HMM.
AFTER THE SUMMER HOLIDAYS, I WILL ARRANGE A SESSION WITH THE SCHOOL COUNSELOR.
I WANT TO HELP YOU, CHERRY. NOT JUST WITH THE COMPULSIVE LYING, BUT WITH YOUR ANGER ISSUES.
I WON'T BE HERE AFTER THE SUMMER HOLIDAYS, MISS JARDINE. MY DAD HAS FALLEN IN LOVE.
WE'RE GOING TO LIVE WITH HIS GIRLFRIEND IN SOMERSET.
IN A BIG HOUSE ON THE EDGE OF A CLIFF!
McBEAN'S CHOCOLATE FACTORY HAS STOPPED MAKING CHOCOLATE TAYSTEE BARS, SO DAD'S LEAVING HIS JOB. HE'S GOING TO MAKE ORGANIC CHOCOLATES!
BYE, BYE, GLASGOW!

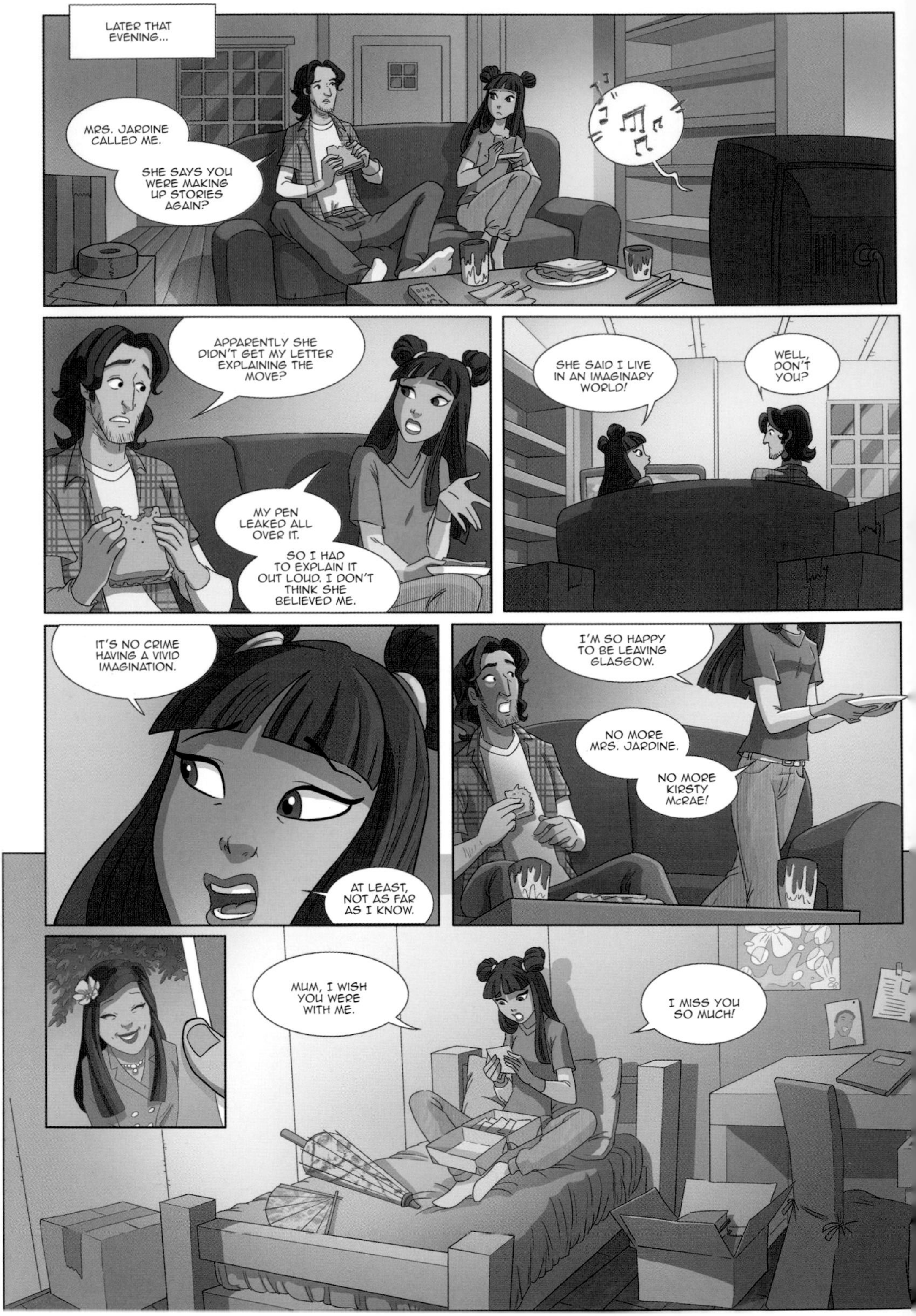
LATER THAT EVENING...
MRS. JARDINE CALLED ME.
SHE SAYS YOU WERE MAKING UP STORIES AGAIN?
APPARENTLY SHE DIDN'T GET MY LETTER EXPLAINING THE MOVE?
MY PEN LEAKED ALL OVER IT.
SO I HAD TO EXPLAIN IT OUT LOUD. I DON'T THINK SHE BELIEVED ME.
SHE SAID I LIVE IN AN IMAGINARY WORLD!
WELL, DON'T YOU?
IT'S NO CRIME HAVING A VIVID IMAGINATION.
AT LEAST, NOT AS FAR AS I KNOW.
I'M SO HAPPY TO BE LEAVING GLASGOW.
NO MORE MRS. JARDINE.
NO MORE KIRSTY McRAE!
MUM, I WISH YOU WERE WITH ME.
I MISS YOU SO MUCH!

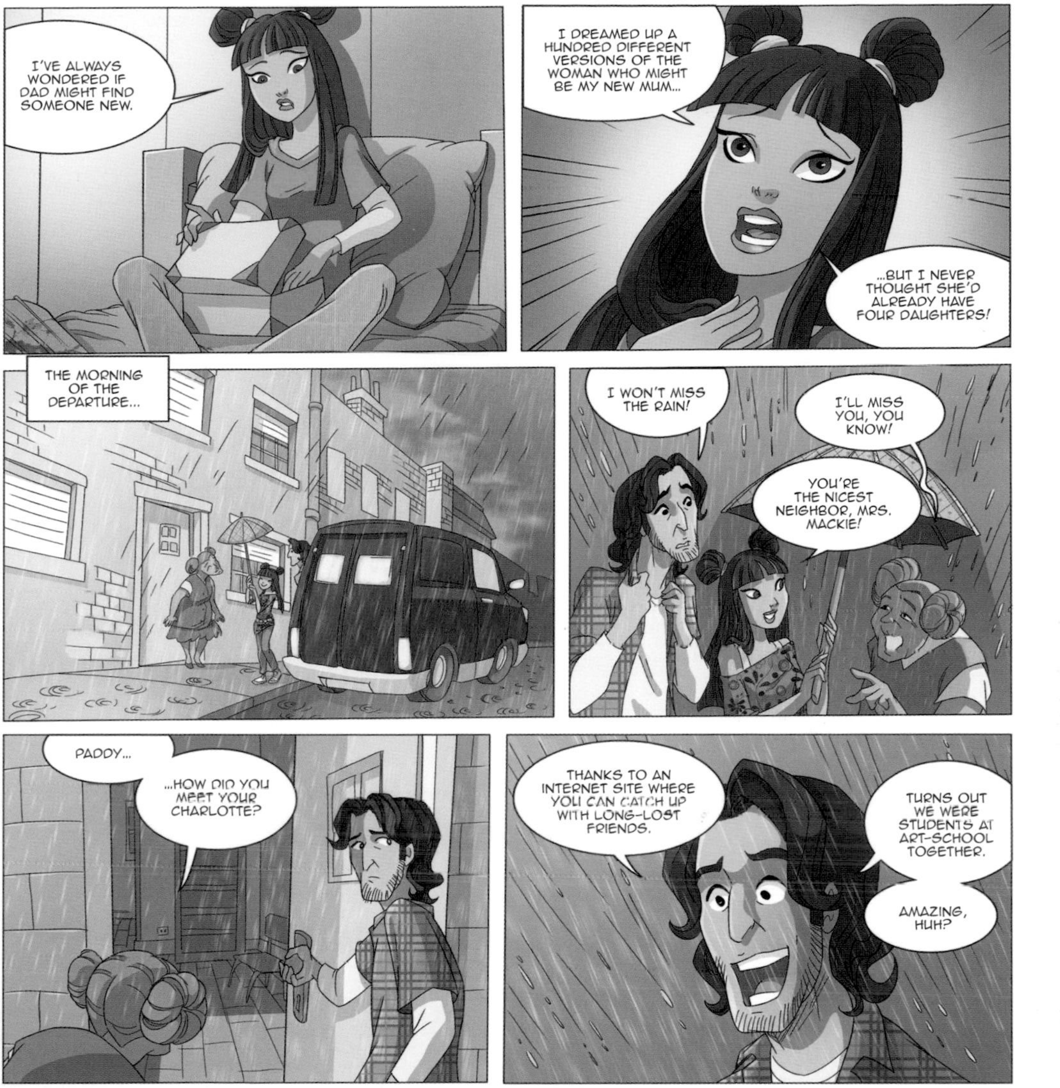
I'VE ALWAYS WONDERED IF DAD MIGHT FIND SOMEONE NEW.
I DREAMED UP A HUNDRED DIFFERENT VERSIONS OF THE WOMAN WHO MIGHT BE MY NEW MUM...
...BUT I NEVER THOUGHT SHE'D ALREADY HAVE FOUR DAUGHTERS!
THE MORNING OF THE DEPARTURE...
I WON'T MISS THE RAIN!
I'LL MISS YOU, YOU KNOW!
YOU'RE THE NICEST NEIGHBOR, MRS. MACKIE!
PADDY...
...HOW DID YOU MEET YOUR CHARLOTTE?
THANKS TO AN INTERNET SITE WHERE YOU CAN CATCH UP WITH LONG-LOST FRIENDS.
TURNS OUT WE WERE STUDENTS AT ART-SCHOOL TOGETHER.
AMAZING, HUH?
CHARLOTTE'S BEEN DIVORCED FOR THREE YEARS AND OPENED A BED & BREAKFAST IN SOMERSET, ENGLAND.
SHE'S COOL.
SHE'S ALREADY BEEN HERE ONCE.
DOWN IN SOMERSET, DAD CAN GET HIS BUSINESS GOING!

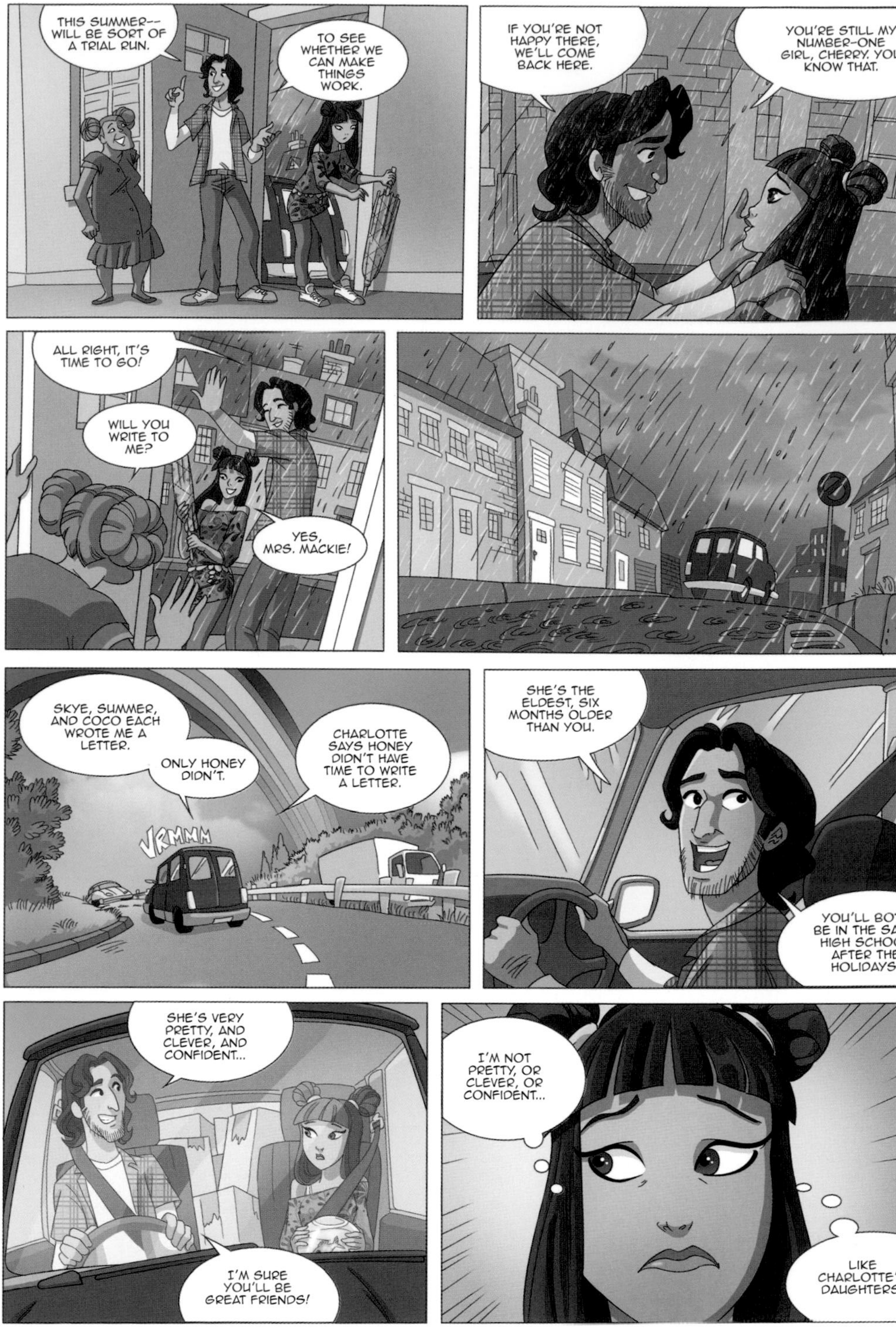
THIS SUMMER-- WILL BE SORT OF A TRIAL RUN.
TO SEE WHETHER WE CAN MAKE THINGS WORK.
IF YOU'RE NOT HAPPY THERE, WE'LL COME BACK HERE.
YOU'RE STILL MY NUMBER-ONE GIRL, CHERRY. YOU KNOW THAT.
ALL RIGHT, IT'S TIME TO GO!
WILL YOU WRITE TO ME?
YES, MRS. MACKIE!
SKYE, SUMMER, AND COCO EACH WROTE ME A LETTER.
ONLY HONEY DIDN'T.
CHARLOTTE SAYS HONEY DIDN'T HAVE TIME TO WRITE A LETTER.
VRMMM
SHE'S THE ELDEST, SIX MONTHS OLDER THAN YOU.
YOU'LL BOTH BE IN THE SAME HIGH SCHOOL AFTER THE HOLIDAYS!
SHE'S VERY PRETTY, AND CLEVER, AND CONFIDENT...
I'M SURE YOU'LL BE GREAT FRIENDS!
I'M NOT PRETTY, OR CLEVER, OR CONFIDENT...
LIKE CHARLOTTE'S DAUGHTERS!

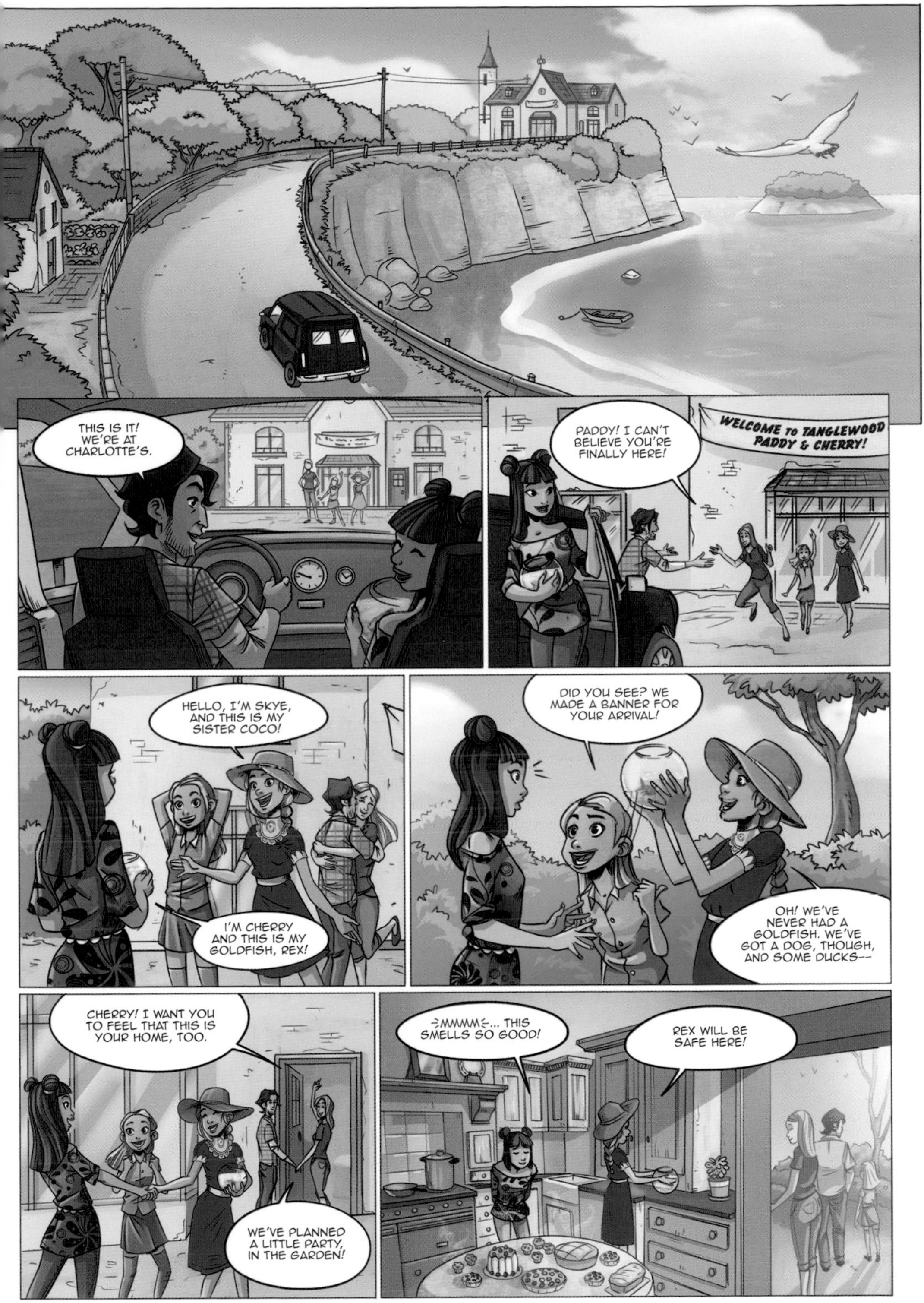
THIS IS IT! WE'RE AT CHARLOTTE'S.
PADDY! I CAN'T BELIEVE YOU'RE FINALLY HERE!
WELCOME TO TANGLEWOOD PADDY & CHERRY!
HELLO, I'M SKYE, AND THIS IS MY SISTER COCO!
I'M CHERRY AND THIS IS MY GOLDFISH, REX!
DID YOU SEE? WE MADE A BANNER FOR YOUR ARRIVAL!
OH! WE'VE NEVER HAD A GOLDFISH. WE'VE GOT A DOG, THOUGH, AND SOME DUCKS--
CHERRY! I WANT YOU TO FEEL THAT THIS IS YOUR HOME, TOO.
WE'VE PLANNED A LITTLE PARTY, IN THE GARDEN!
MMMM... THIS SMELLS SO GOOD!
REX WILL BE SAFE HERE!

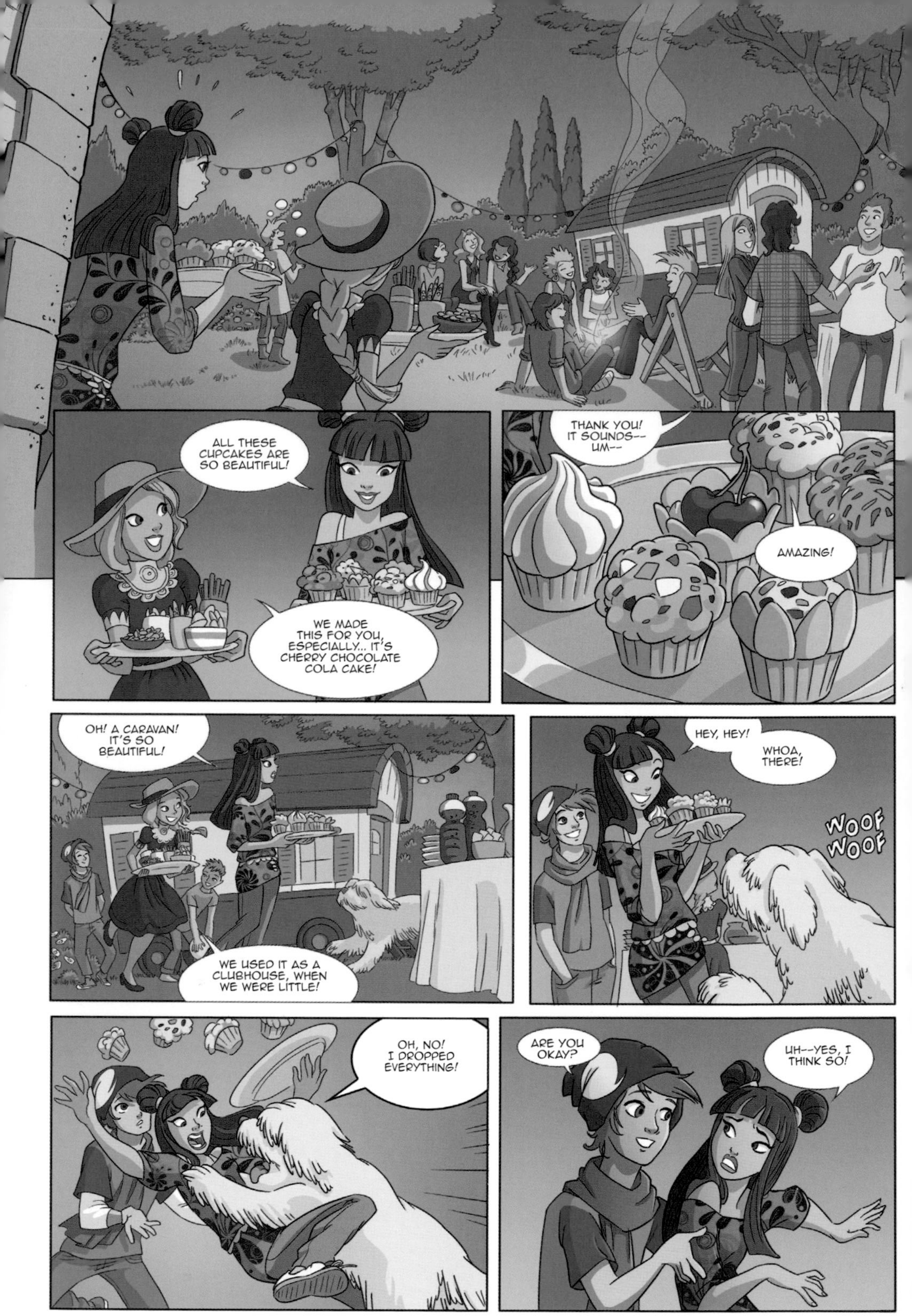
ALL THESE CUPCAKES ARE SO BEAUTIFUL!
WE MADE THIS FOR YOU, ESPECIALLY... IT'S CHERRY CHOCOLATE COLA CAKE!
THANK YOU! IT SOUNDS-- UM--
AMAZING!
OH! A CARAVAN! IT'S SO BEAUTIFUL!
WE USED IT AS A CLUBHOUSE, WHEN WE WERE LITTLE!
HEY, HEY!
WHOA, THERE!
WOOF WOOF
OH, NO! I DROPPED EVERYTHING!
ARE YOU OKAY?
UH--YES, I THINK SO!

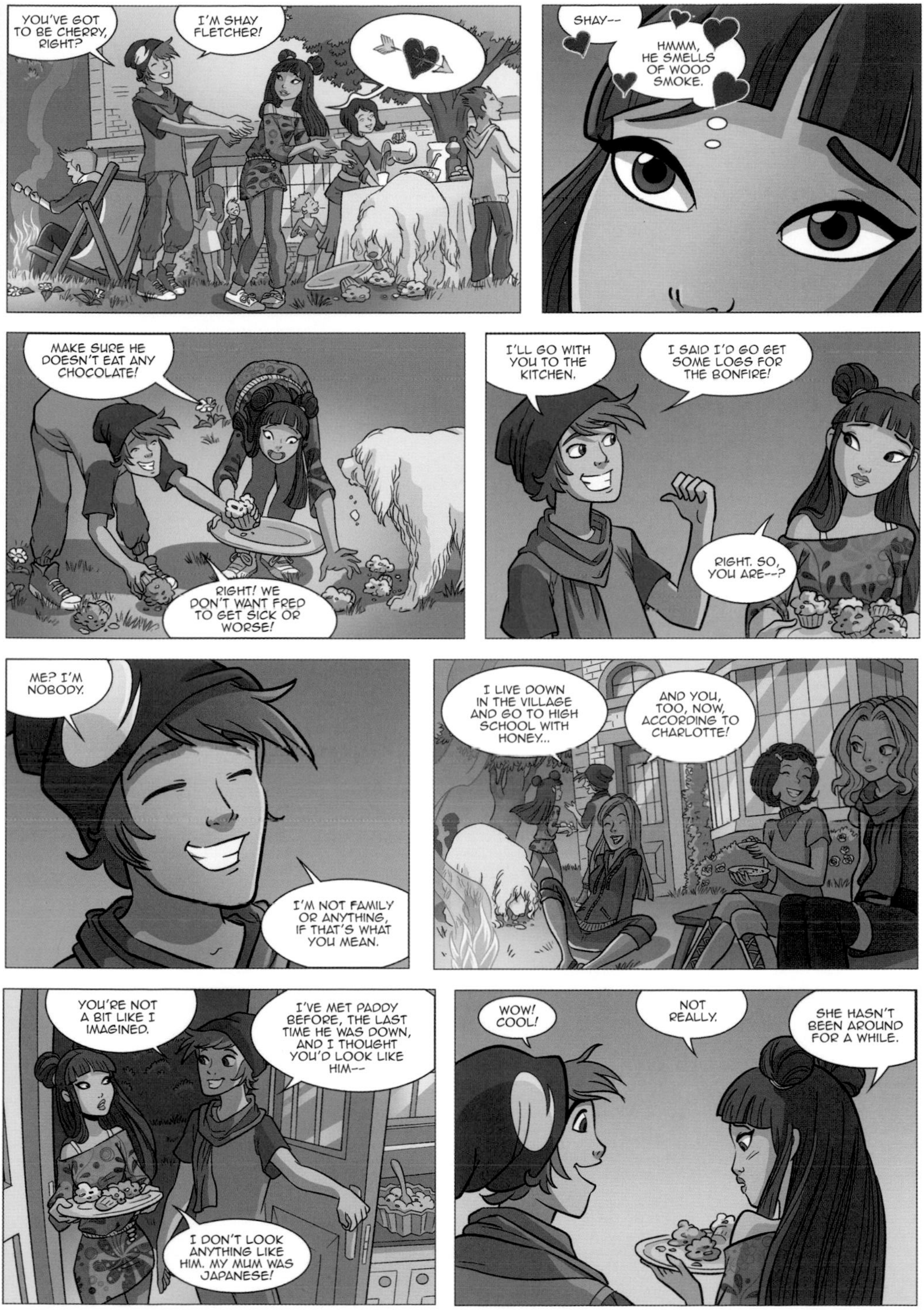
YOU'VE GOT TO BE CHERRY, RIGHT?
I'M SHAY FLETCHER!
SHAY--
HMMM, HE SMELLS OF WOOD SMOKE.
MAKE SURE HE DOESN'T EAT ANY CHOCOLATE!
RIGHT! WE DON'T WANT FRED TO GET SICK OR WORSE!
I SAID I'D GO GET SOME LOGS FOR THE BONFIRE!
I'LL GO WITH YOU TO THE KITCHEN.
RIGHT. SO, YOU ARE--?
ME? I'M NOBODY.
I'M NOT FAMILY OR ANYTHING, IF THAT'S WHAT YOU MEAN.
I LIVE DOWN IN THE VILLAGE AND GO TO HIGH SCHOOL WITH HONEY...
AND YOU, TOO, NOW, ACCORDING TO CHARLOTTE!
YOU'RE NOT A BIT LIKE I IMAGINED.
I'VE MET PADDY BEFORE, THE LAST TIME HE WAS DOWN, AND I THOUGHT YOU'D LOOK LIKE HIM--
I DON'T LOOK ANYTHING LIKE HIM. MY MUM WAS JAPANESE!
WOW! COOL!
NOT REALLY.
SHE HASN'T BEEN AROUND FOR A WHILE.

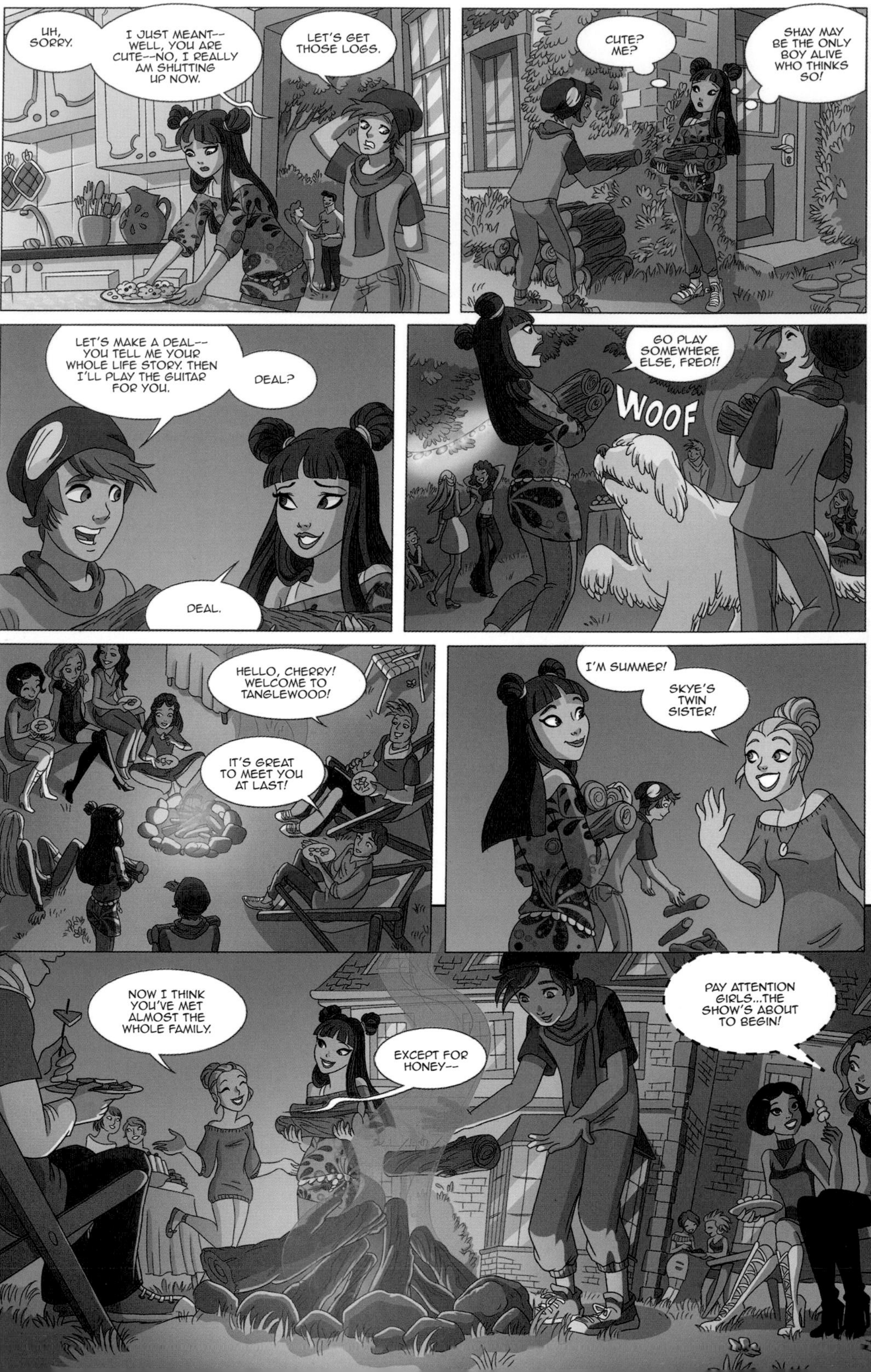
UH, SORRY.
I JUST MEANT-- WELL, YOU ARE CUTE--NO, I REALLY AM SHUTTING UP NOW.
LET'S GET THOSE LOGS.
CUTE? ME?
SHAY MAY BE THE ONLY BOY ALIVE WHO THINKS SO!
LET'S MAKE A DEAL-- YOU TELL ME YOUR WHOLE LIFE STORY. THEN I'LL PLAY THE GUITAR FOR YOU.
DEAL?
DEAL.
GO PLAY SOMEWHERE ELSE, FRED!!
WOOF
HELLO, CHERRY! WELCOME TO TANGLEWOOD!
IT'S GREAT TO MEET YOU AT LAST!
I'M SUMMER!
SKYE'S TWIN SISTER!
NOW I THINK YOU'VE MET ALMOST THE WHOLE FAMILY.
EXCEPT FOR HONEY--
PAY ATTENTION GIRLS...THE SHOW'S ABOUT TO BEGIN!

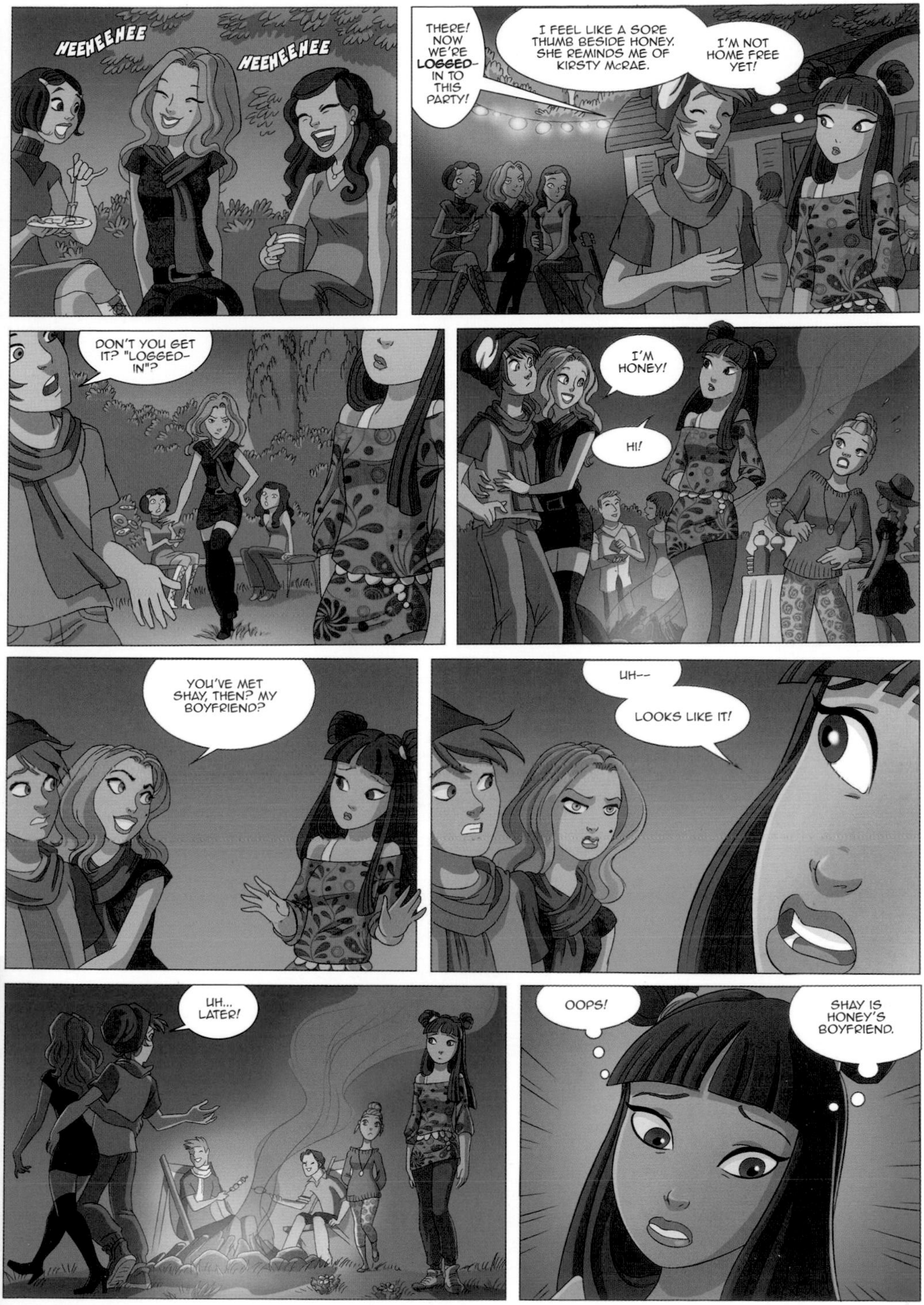

HEEHEEHEE
HEEHEEHEE
THERE! NOW WE'RE LOGGED-IN TO THIS PARTY!
I FEEL LIKE A SORE THUMB BESIDE HONEY. SHE REMINDS ME OF KIRSTY McRAE.
I'M NOT HOME FREE YET!
DON'T YOU GET IT? "LOGGED-IN"?
I'M HONEY!
HI!
YOU'VE MET SHAY, THEN? MY BOYFRIEND?
UH--
LOOKS LIKE IT!
UH... LATER!
OOPS!
SHAY IS HONEY'S BOYFRIEND.

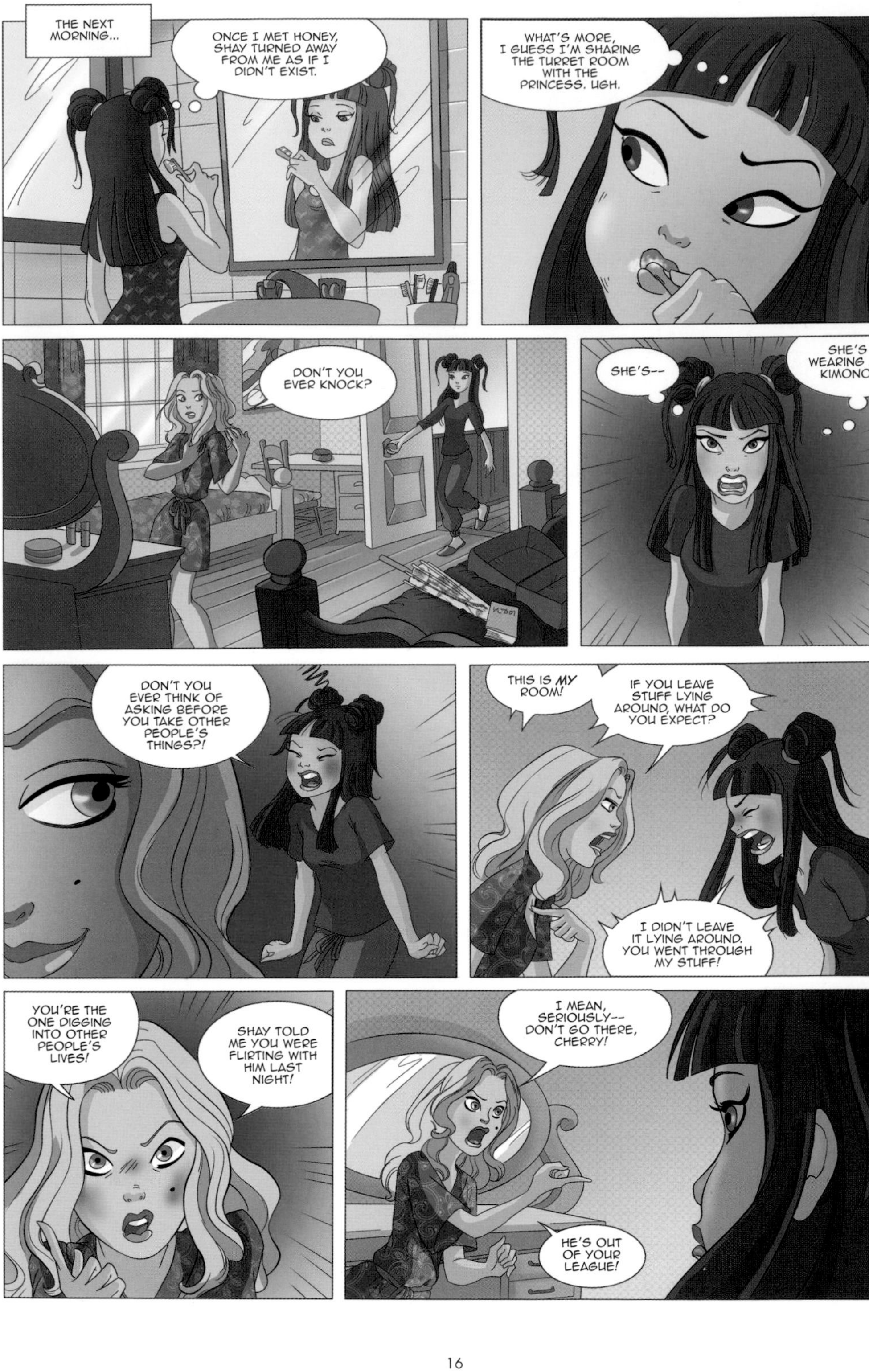
THE NEXT MORNING...
ONCE I MET HONEY, SHAY TURNED AWAY FROM ME AS IF I DIDN'T EXIST.
WHAT'S MORE, I GUESS I'M SHARING THE TURRET ROOM WITH THE PRINCESS. UGH.
DON'T YOU EVER KNOCK?
SHE'S--
SHE'S WEARING MY KIMONO!
DON'T YOU EVER THINK OF ASKING BEFORE YOU TAKE OTHER PEOPLE'S THINGS?!
THIS IS MY ROOM!
IF YOU LEAVE STUFF LYING AROUND, WHAT DO YOU EXPECT?
I DIDN'T LEAVE IT LYING AROUND. YOU WENT THROUGH MY STUFF!
YOU'RE THE ONE DIGGING INTO OTHER PEOPLE'S LIVES!
SHAY TOLD ME YOU WERE FLIRTING WITH HIM LAST NIGHT!
I MEAN, SERIOUSLY-- DON'T GO THERE, CHERRY!
HE'S OUT OF YOUR LEAGUE!

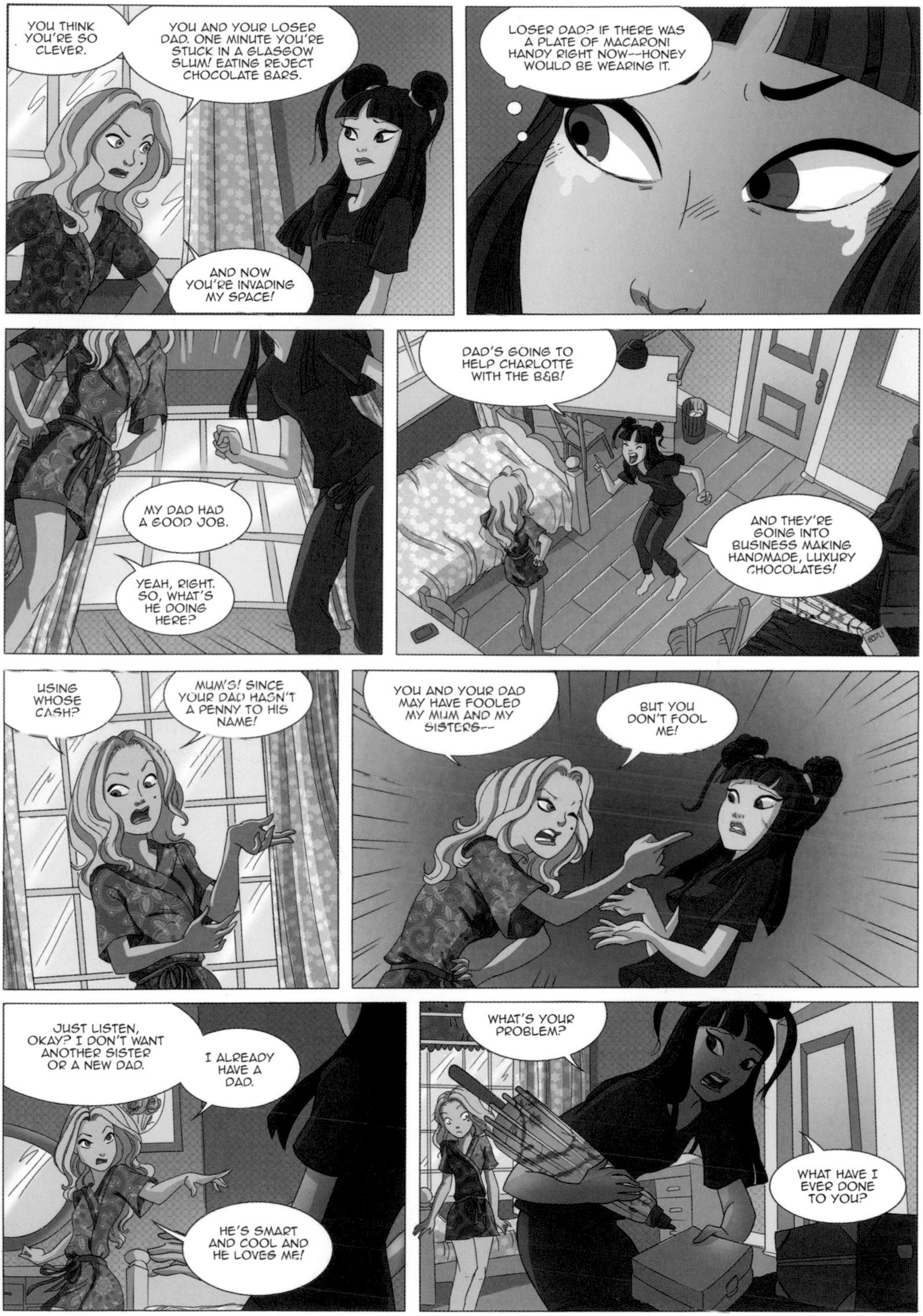
YOU THINK YOU'RE SO CLEVER.
YOU AND YOUR LOSER DAD. ONE MINUTE YOU'RE STUCK IN A GLASGOW SLUM! EATING REJECT CHOCOLATE BARS.
AND NOW YOU'RE INVADING MY SPACE!
LOSER DAD? IF THERE WAS A PLATE OF MACARONI HANDY RIGHT NOW--HONEY WOULD BE WEARING IT.
MY DAD HAD A GOOD JOB.
YEAH, RIGHT. SO, WHAT'S HE DOING HERE?
DAD'S GOING TO HELP CHARLOTTE WITH THE B&B!
AND THEY'RE GOING INTO BUSINESS MAKING HANDMADE, LUXURY CHOCOLATES!
USING WHOSE CASH?
MUM'S! SINCE YOUR DAD HASN'T A PENNY TO HIS NAME!
YOU AND YOUR DAD MAY HAVE FOOLED MY MUM AND MY SISTERS--
BUT YOU DON'T FOOL ME!
JUST LISTEN, OKAY? I DON'T WANT ANOTHER SISTER OR A NEW DAD.
I ALREADY HAVE A DAD.
HE'S SMART AND COOL AND HE LOVES ME!
WHAT'S YOUR PROBLEM?
WHAT HAVE I EVER DONE TO YOU?

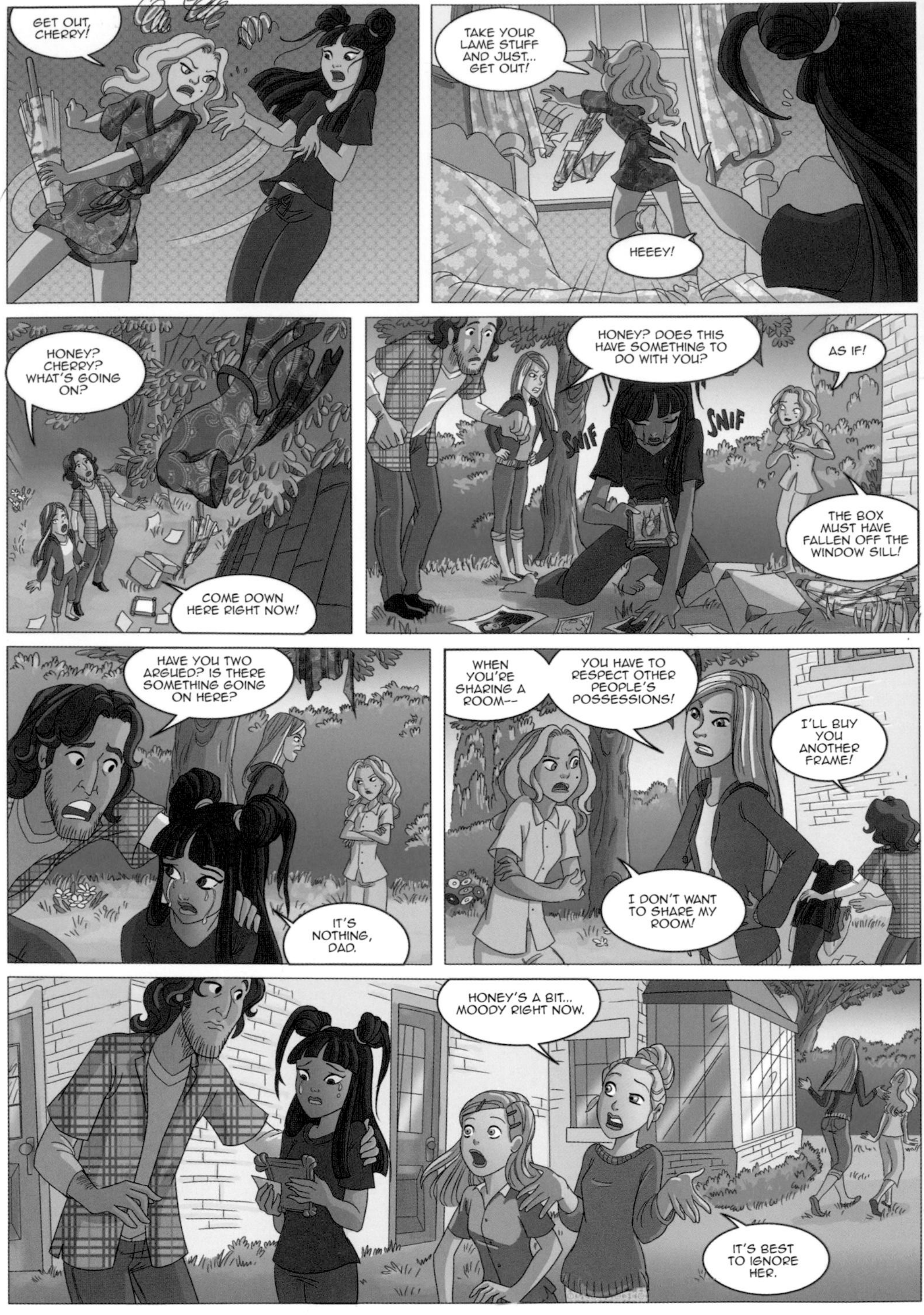
GET OUT, CHERRY!
TAKE YOUR LAME STUFF AND JUST... GET OUT!
HEEEY!
HONEY? CHERRY? WHAT'S GOING ON?
COME DOWN HERE RIGHT NOW!
HONEY? DOES THIS HAVE SOMETHING TO DO WITH YOU?
AS IF!
SNIF
SNIF
THE BOX MUST HAVE FALLEN OFF THE WINDOW SILL!
HAVE YOU TWO ARGUED? IS THERE SOMETHING GOING ON HERE?
IT'S NOTHING, DAD.
WHEN YOU'RE SHARING A ROOM--
YOU HAVE TO RESPECT OTHER PEOPLE'S POSSESSIONS!
I'LL BUY YOU ANOTHER FRAME!
I DON'T WANT TO SHARE MY ROOM!
HONEY'S A BIT... MOODY RIGHT NOW.
IT'S BEST TO IGNORE HER.

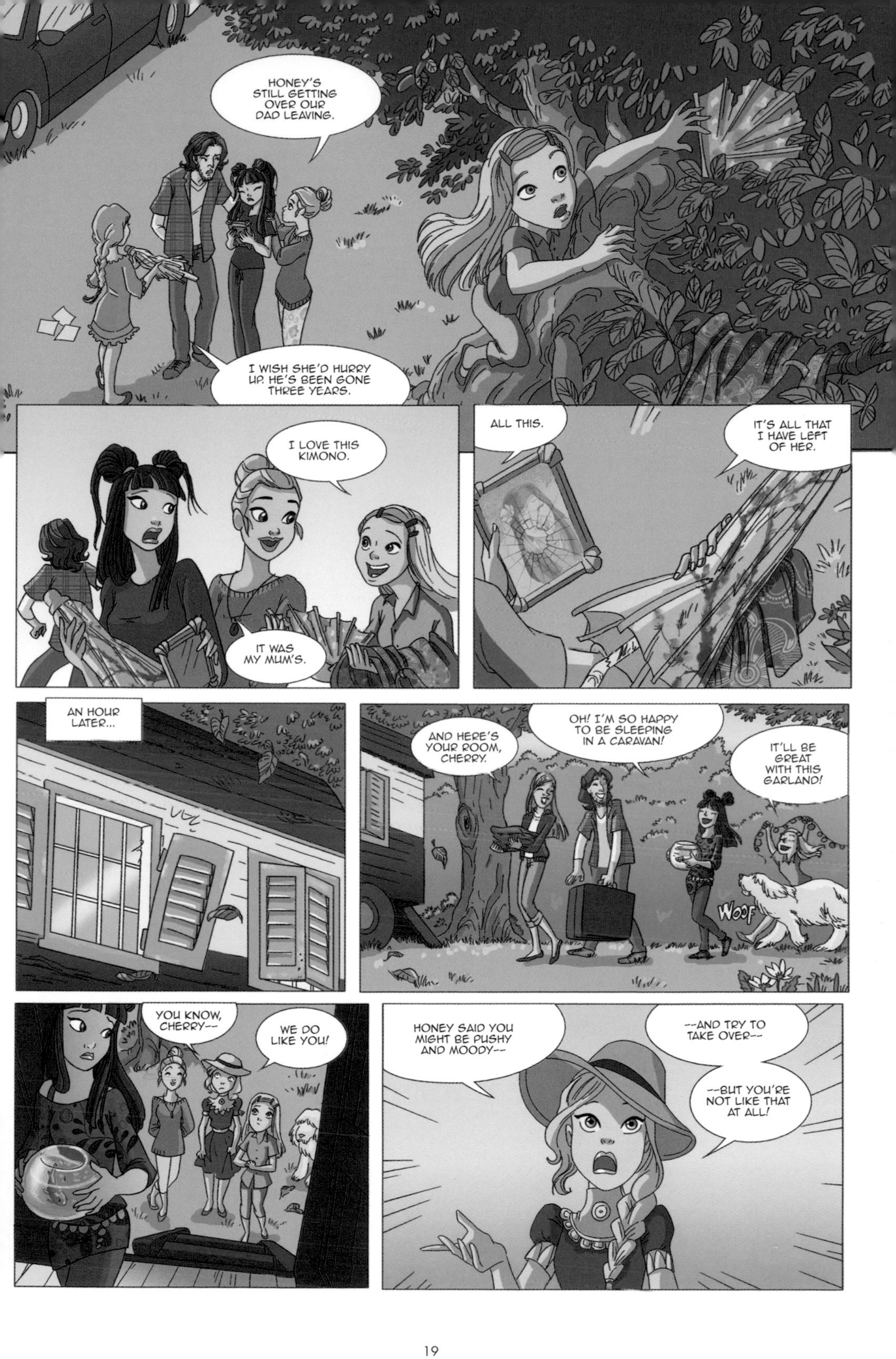
HONEY'S STILL GETTING OVER OUR DAD LEAVING.
I WISH SHE'D HURRY UP. HE'S BEEN GONE THREE YEARS.
I LOVE THIS KIMONO.
IT WAS MY MUM'S.
ALL THIS.
IT'S ALL THAT I HAVE LEFT OF HER.
AN HOUR LATER...
AND HERE'S YOUR ROOM, CHERRY.
OH! I'M SO HAPPY TO BE SLEEPING IN A CARAVAN!
IT'LL BE GREAT WITH THIS GARLAND!
WOOF
YOU KNOW, CHERRY--
WE DO LIKE YOU!
HONEY SAID YOU MIGHT BE PUSHY AND MOODY--
--AND TRY TO TAKE OVER--
--BUT YOU'RE NOT LIKE THAT AT ALL!

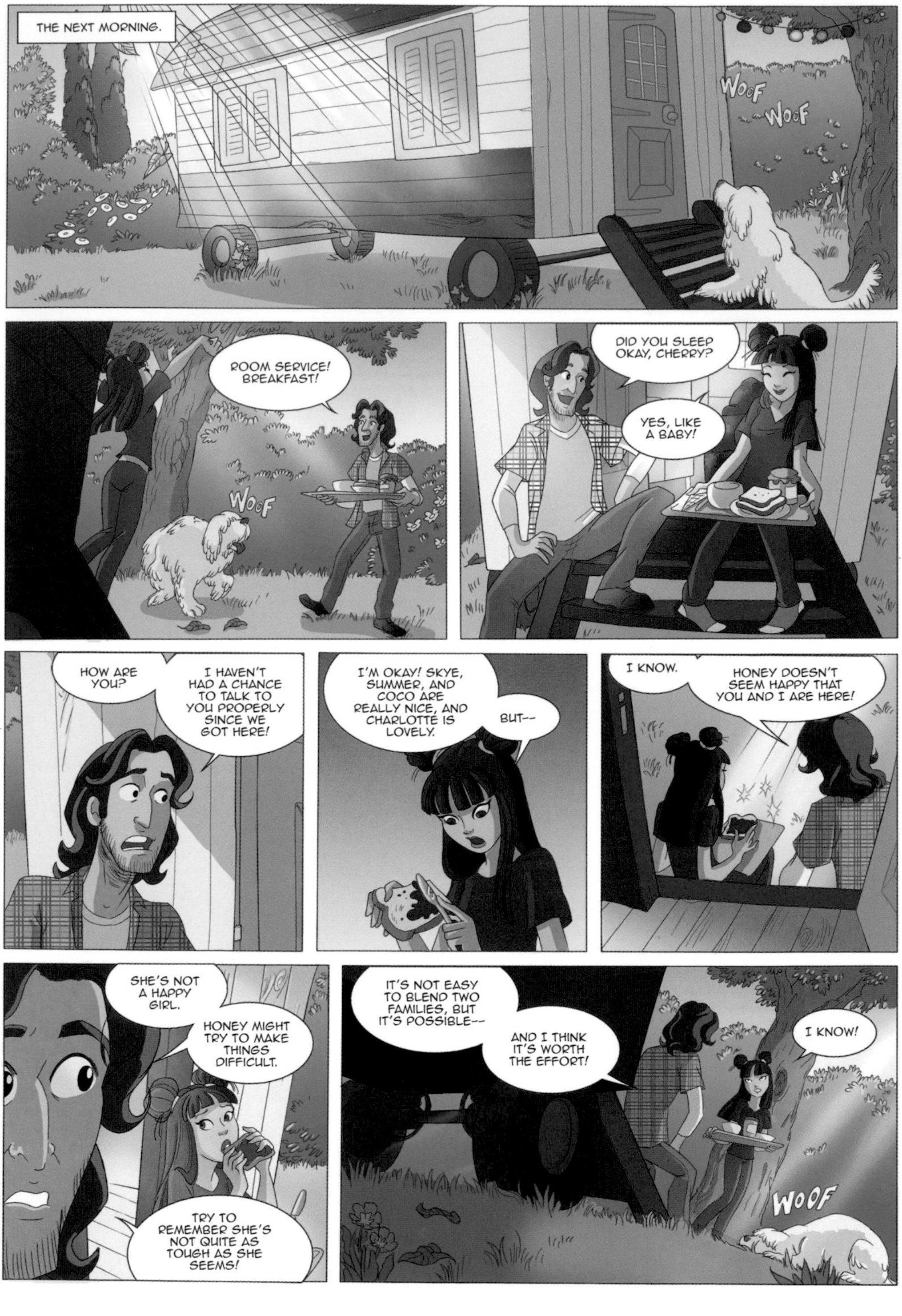
THE NEXT MORNING.
WOOF
WOOF
ROOM SERVICE! BREAKFAST!
WOOF
DID YOU SLEEP OKAY, CHERRY?
YES, LIKE A BABY!
HOW ARE YOU?
I HAVEN'T HAD A CHANCE TO TALK TO YOU PROPERLY SINCE WE GOT HERE!
I'M OKAY! SKYE, SUMMER, AND COCO ARE REALLY NICE, AND CHARLOTTE IS LOVELY.
BUT--
I KNOW.
HONEY DOESN'T SEEM HAPPY THAT YOU AND I ARE HERE!
SHE'S NOT A HAPPY GIRL.
HONEY MIGHT TRY TO MAKE THINGS DIFFICULT.
TRY TO REMEMBER SHE'S NOT QUITE AS TOUGH AS SHE SEEMS!
IT'S NOT EASY TO BLEND TWO FAMILIES, BUT IT'S POSSIBLE--
AND I THINK IT'S WORTH THE EFFORT!
I KNOW!
WOOF

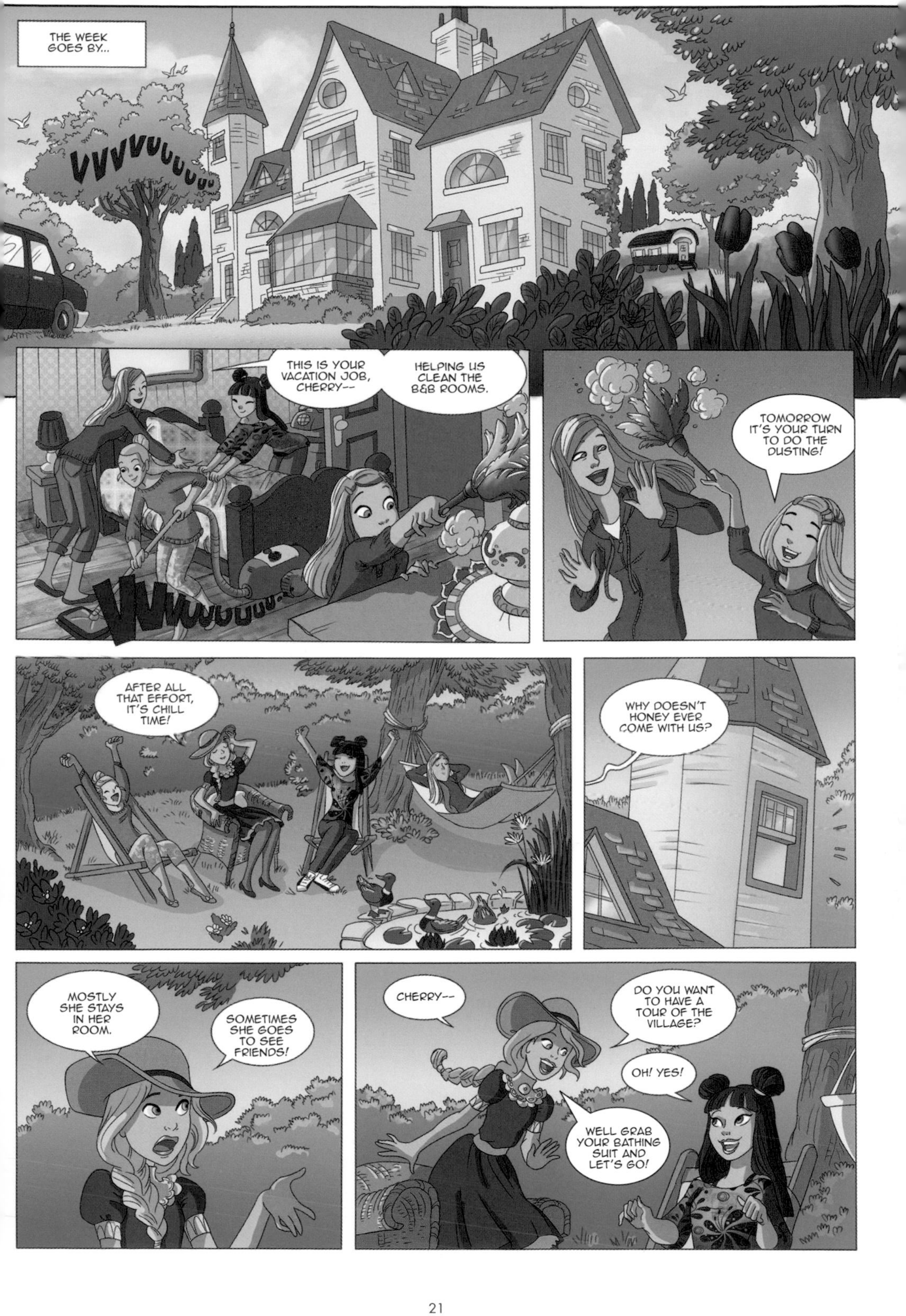

THE WEEK GOES BY...
VVVVUUUUUU
THIS IS YOUR VACATION JOB, CHERRY--
HELPING US CLEAN THE B&B ROOMS.
VVVUUUUUUU
TOMORROW IT'S YOUR TURN TO DO THE DUSTING!
AFTER ALL THAT EFFORT, IT'S CHILL TIME!
WHY DOESN'T HONEY EVER COME WITH US?
MOSTLY SHE STAYS IN HER ROOM.
SOMETIMES SHE GOES TO SEE FRIENDS!
CHERRY--
DO YOU WANT TO HAVE A TOUR OF THE VILLAGE?
OH! YES!
WELL GRAB YOUR BATHING SUIT AND LET'S GO!

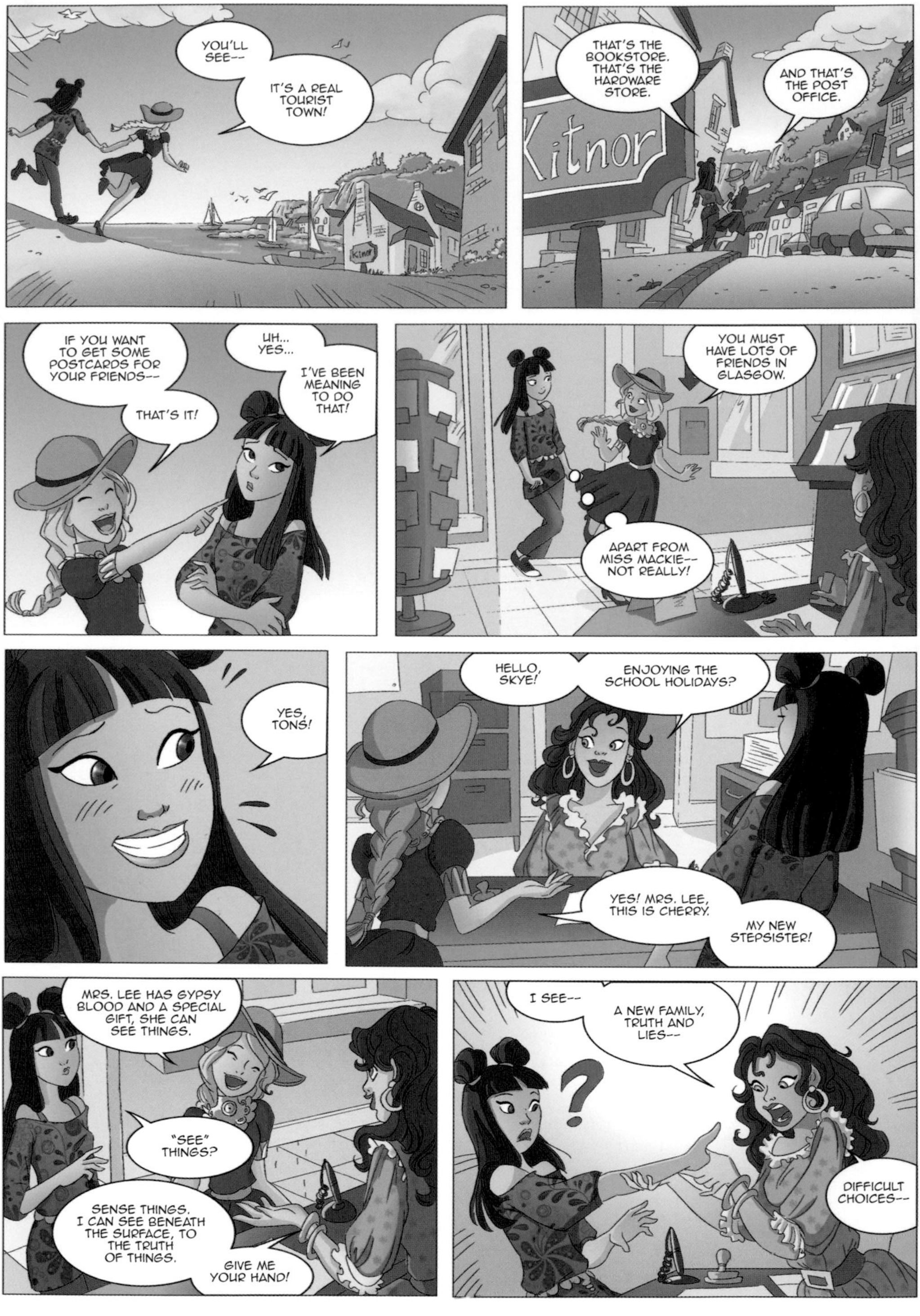
YOU'LL SEE--
IT'S A REAL TOURIST TOWN!
Kitnor
THAT'S THE BOOKSTORE. THAT'S THE HARDWARE STORE.
AND THAT'S THE POST OFFICE.
IF YOU WANT TO GET SOME POSTCARDS FOR YOUR FRIENDS--
THAT'S IT!
UH... YES...
I'VE BEEN MEANING TO DO THAT!
YOU MUST HAVE LOTS OF FRIENDS IN GLASGOW.
APART FROM MISS MACKIE-- NOT REALLY!
YES, TONS!
HELLO, SKYE!
ENJOYING THE SCHOOL HOLIDAYS?
YES! MRS. LEE, THIS IS CHERRY.
MY NEW STEPSISTER!
MRS. LEE HAS GYPSY BLOOD AND A SPECIAL GIFT, SHE CAN SEE THINGS.
"SEE" THINGS?
SENSE THINGS. I CAN SEE BENEATH THE SURFACE, TO THE TRUTH OF THINGS.
GIVE ME YOUR HAND!
I SEE--
A NEW FAMILY, TRUTH AND LIES--
?
DIFFICULT CHOICES--

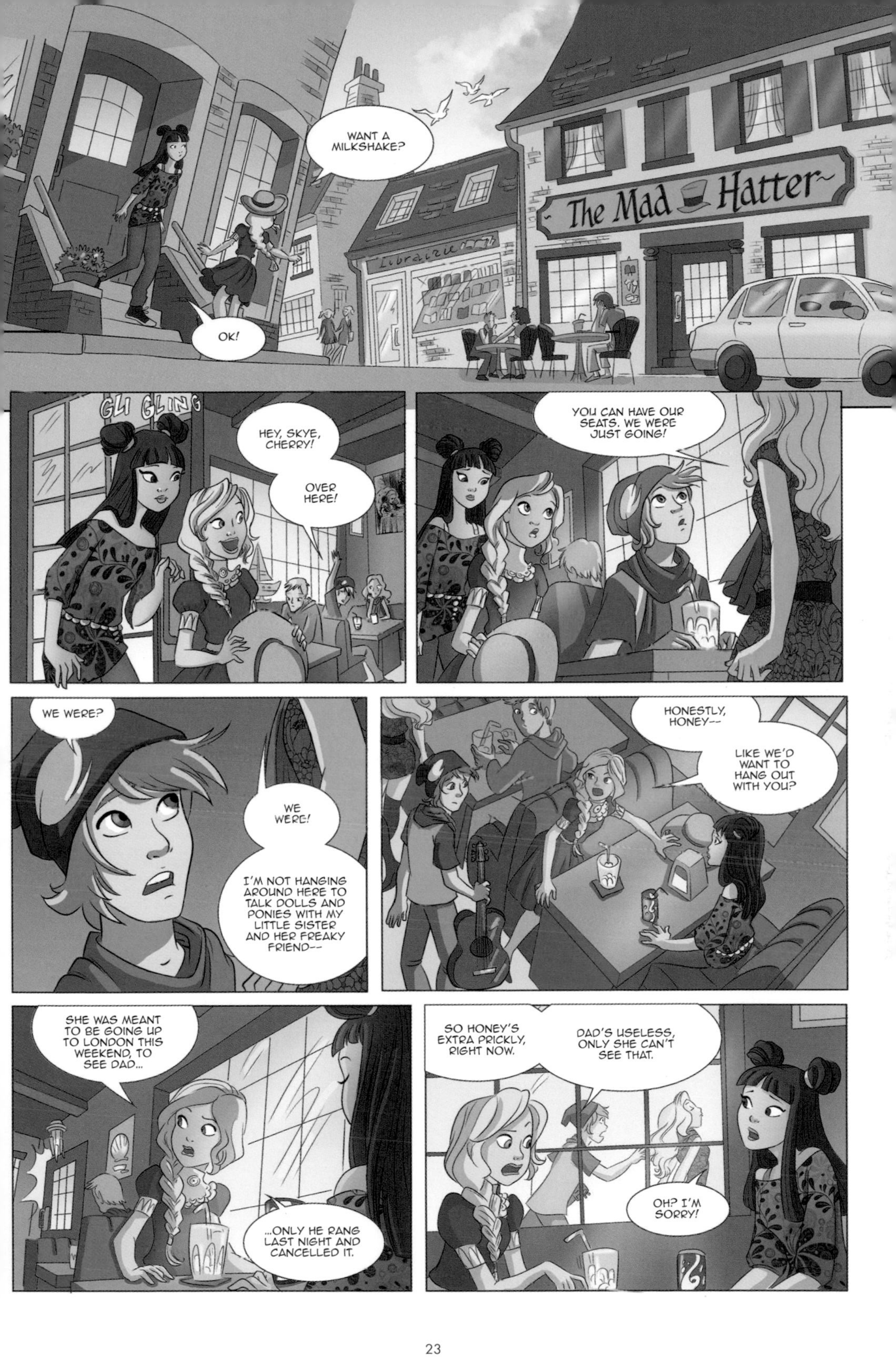
The Mad Hatter
Librairie
WANT A MILKSHAKE?
OK!
GLI GLING
HEY, SKYE, CHERRY!
OVER HERE!
YOU CAN HAVE OUR SEATS. WE WERE JUST GOING!
WE WERE?
WE WERE!
I'M NOT HANGING AROUND HERE TO TALK DOLLS AND PONIES WITH MY LITTLE SISTER AND HER FREAKY FRIEND--
HONESTLY, HONEY--
LIKE WE'D WANT TO HANG OUT WITH YOU?
SHE WAS MEANT TO BE GOING UP TO LONDON THIS WEEKEND, TO SEE DAD...
...ONLY HE RANG LAST NIGHT AND CANCELLED IT.
SO HONEY'S EXTRA PRICKLY, RIGHT NOW.
DAD'S USELESS, ONLY SHE CAN'T SEE THAT.
OH? I'M SORRY!

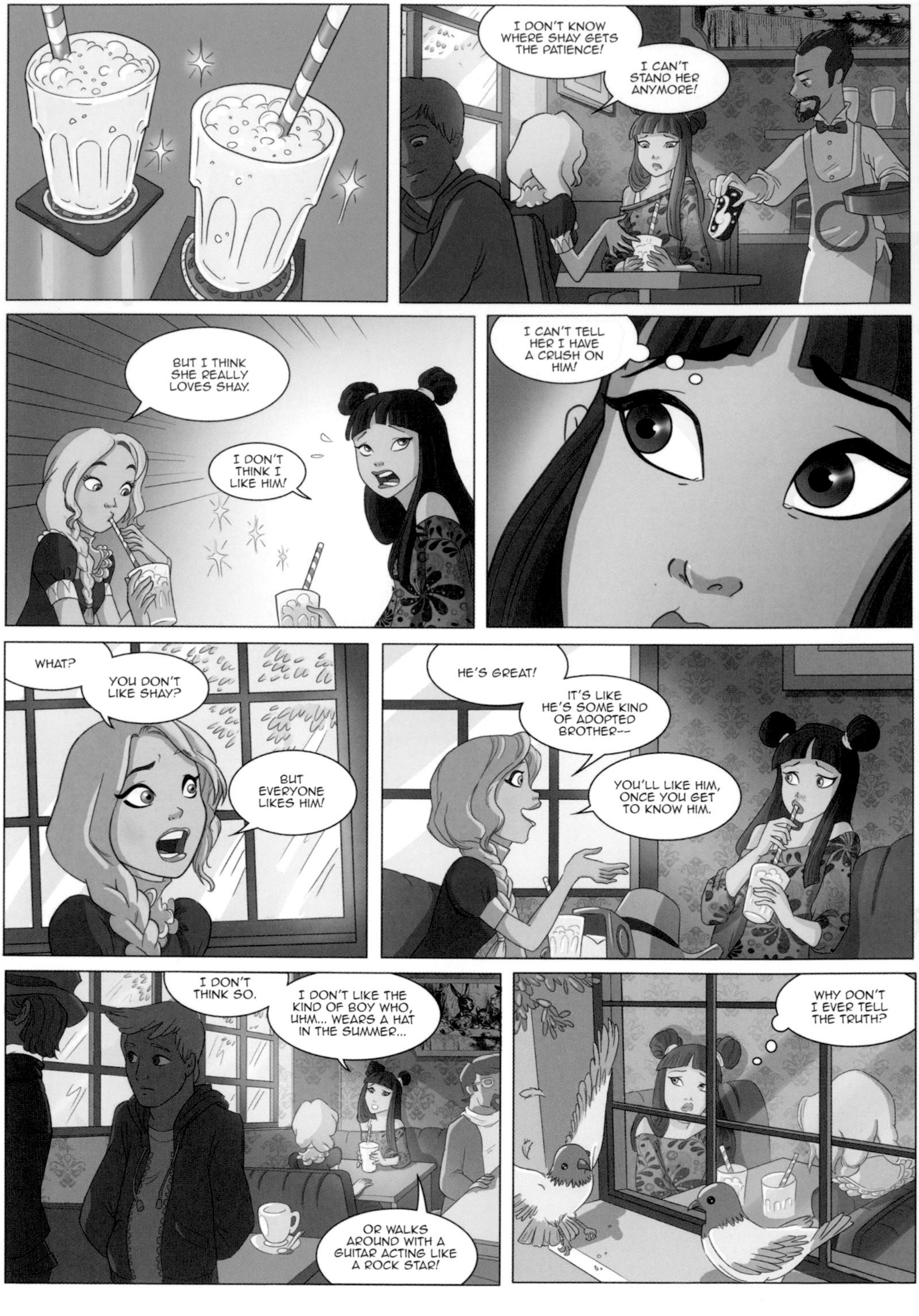
I DON'T KNOW WHERE SHAY GETS THE PATIENCE!
I CAN'T STAND HER ANYMORE!
BUT I THINK SHE REALLY LOVES SHAY.
I DON'T THINK I LIKE HIM!
I CAN'T TELL HER I HAVE A CRUSH ON HIM!
WHAT?
YOU DON'T LIKE SHAY?
BUT EVERYONE LIKES HIM!
HE'S GREAT!
IT'S LIKE HE'S SOME KIND OF ADOPTED BROTHER--
YOU'LL LIKE HIM, ONCE YOU GET TO KNOW HIM.
I DON'T THINK SO.
I DON'T LIKE THE KIND OF BOY WHO, UHM... WEARS A HAT IN THE SUMMER...
OR WALKS AROUND WITH A GUITAR ACTING LIKE A ROCK STAR!
WHY DON'T I EVER TELL THE TRUTH?

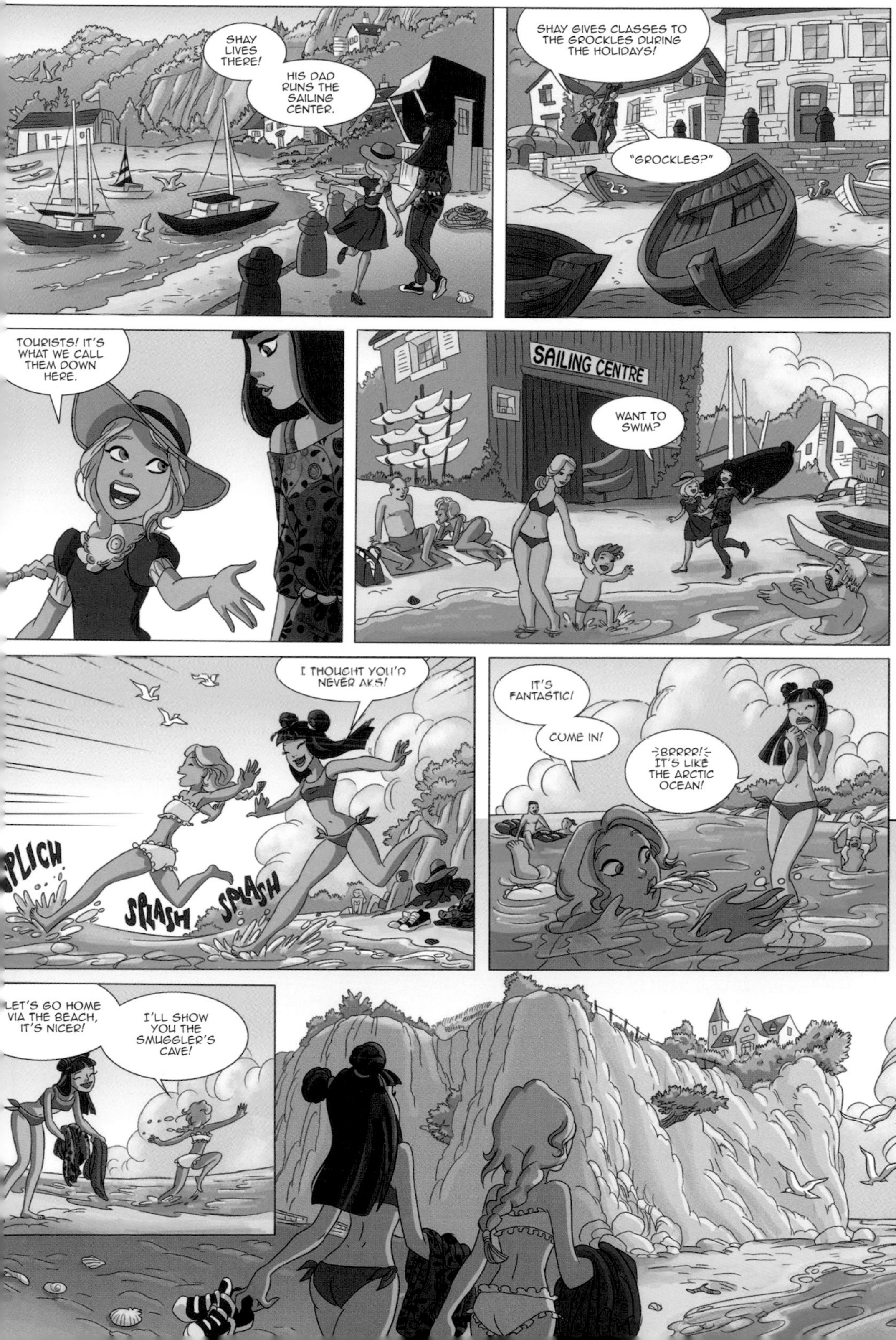
SHAY LIVES THERE!
HIS DAD RUNS THE SAILING CENTER.
SHAY GIVES CLASSES TO THE GROCKLES DURING THE HOLIDAYS!
"GROCKLES?"
23
TOURISTS! IT'S WHAT WE CALL THEM DOWN HERE.
SAILING CENTRE
WANT TO SWIM?
I THOUGHT YOU'D NEVER AKS!
PLICH
SPLASH
SPLASH
IT'S FANTASTIC!
COME IN!
BRRRR! IT'S LIKE THE ARCTIC OCEAN!
LET'S GO HOME VIA THE BEACH, IT'S NICER!
I'LL SHOW YOU THE SMUGGLER'S CAVE!

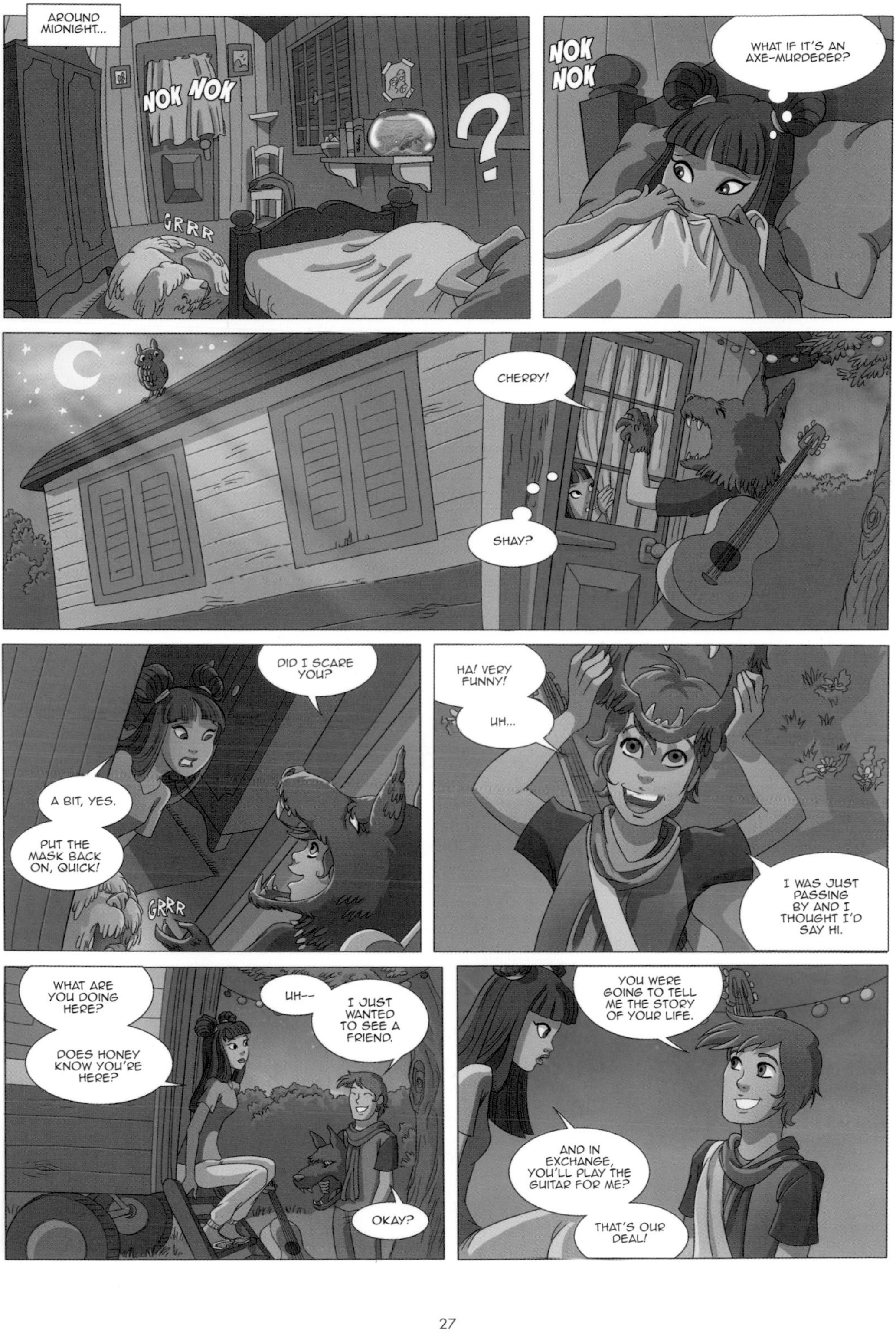

AROUND MIDNIGHT...
NOK NOK
GRRR
?
NOK NOK
WHAT IF IT'S AN AXE-MURDERER?
CHERRY!
SHAY?
DID I SCARE YOU?
A BIT, YES.
PUT THE MASK BACK ON, QUICK!
GRRR
HA! VERY FUNNY!
UH...
I WAS JUST PASSING BY AND I THOUGHT I'D SAY HI.
WHAT ARE YOU DOING HERE?
DOES HONEY KNOW YOU'RE HERE?
UH--
I JUST WANTED TO SEE A FRIEND.
OKAY?
YOU WERE GOING TO TELL ME THE STORY OF YOUR LIFE.
AND IN EXCHANGE, YOU'LL PLAY THE GUITAR FOR ME?
THAT'S OUR DEAL!

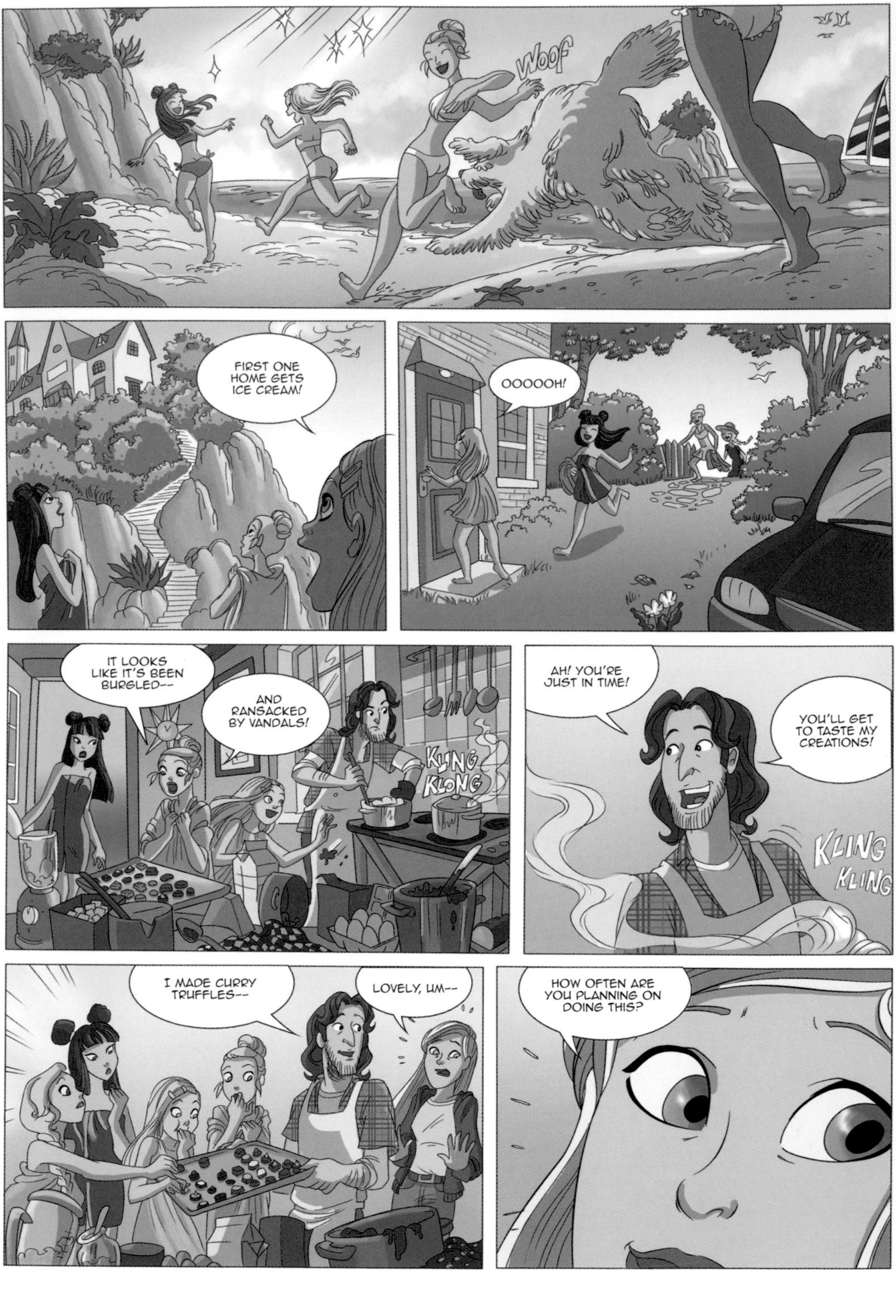
WOOF
FIRST ONE HOME GETS ICE CREAM!
OOOOOH!
IT LOOKS LIKE IT'S BEEN BURGLED--
AND RANSACKED BY VANDALS!
KLING KLONG
AH! YOU'RE JUST IN TIME!
YOU'LL GET TO TASTE MY CREATIONS!
KLING KLING
I MADE CURRY TRUFFLES--
LOVELY, UM--
HOW OFTEN ARE YOU PLANNING ON DOING THIS?

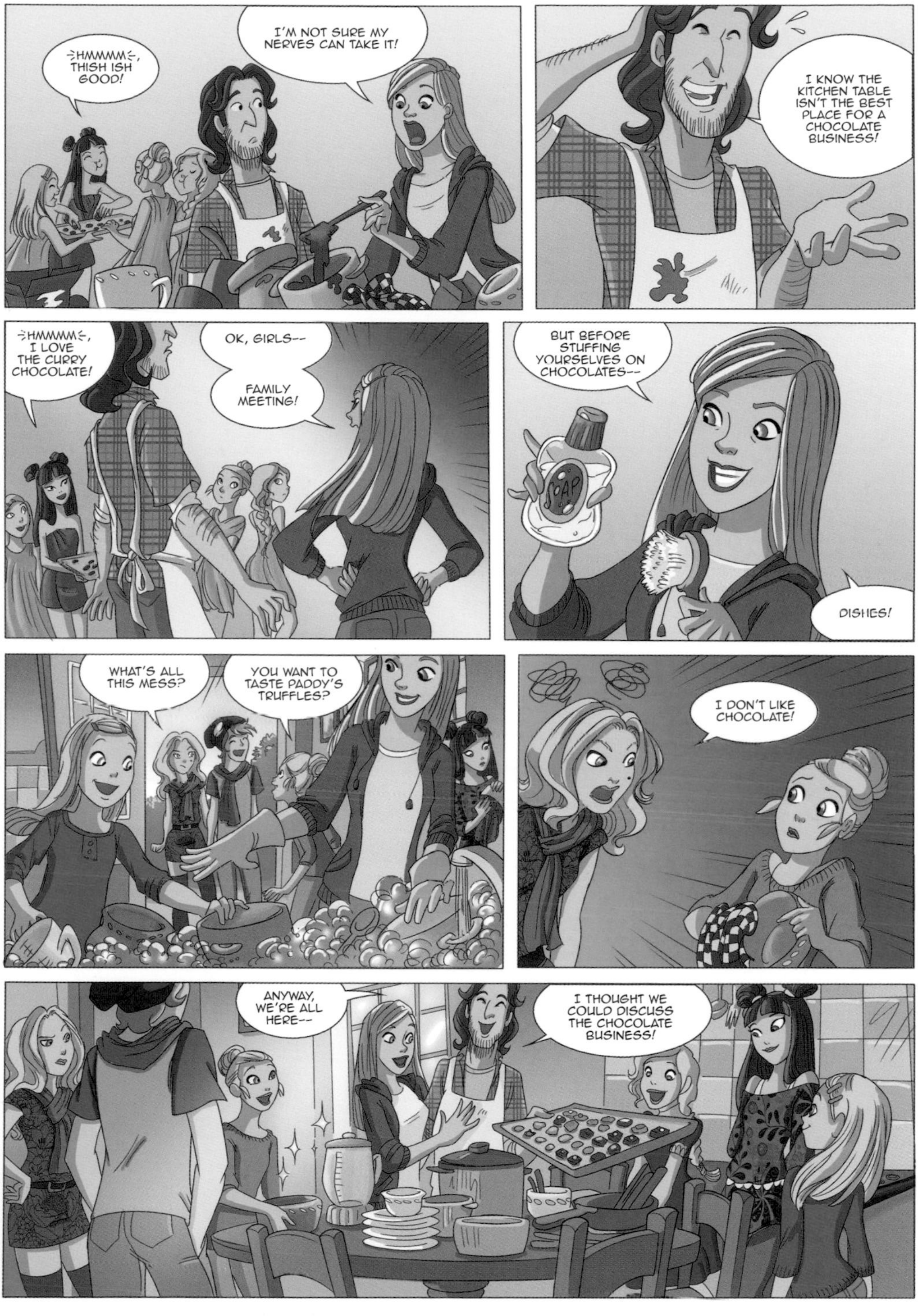

≑HMMMM≑, THISH ISH GOOD!
I'M NOT SURE MY NERVES CAN TAKE IT!
I KNOW THE KITCHEN TABLE ISN'T THE BEST PLACE FOR A CHOCOLATE BUSINESS!
≑HMMMM≑, I LOVE THE CURRY CHOCOLATE!
OK, GIRLS--
FAMILY MEETING!
BUT BEFORE STUFFING YOURSELVES ON CHOCOLATES--
SOAP
DISHES!
WHAT'S ALL THIS MESS?
YOU WANT TO TASTE PADDY'S TRUFFLES?
I DON'T LIKE CHOCOLATE!
ANYWAY, WE'RE ALL HERE--
I THOUGHT WE COULD DISCUSS THE CHOCOLATE BUSINESS!

33

34

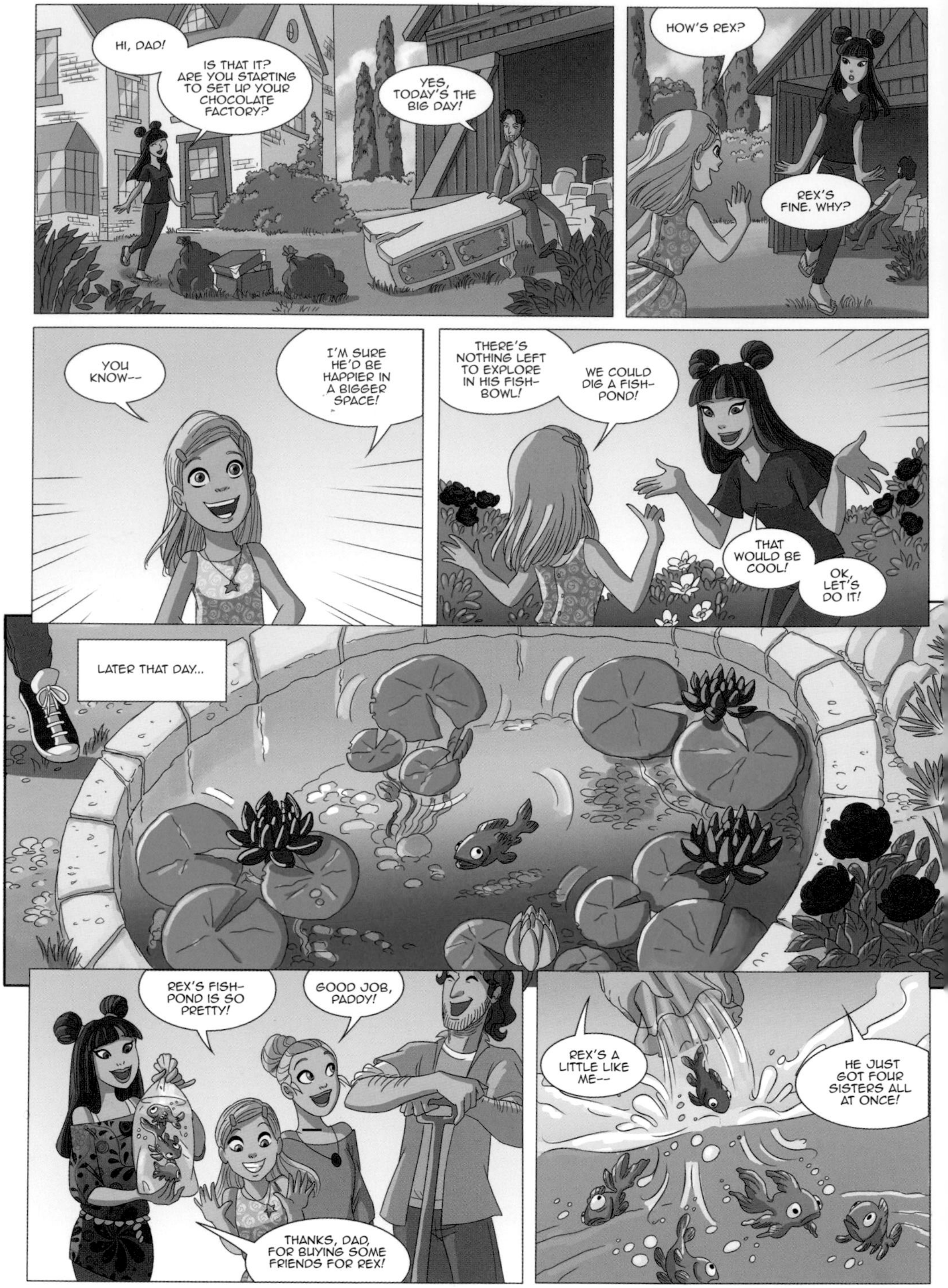
HI, DAD!
IS THAT IT? ARE YOU STARTING TO SET UP YOUR CHOCOLATE FACTORY?
YES, TODAY'S THE BIG DAY!
HOW'S REX?
REX'S FINE. WHY?
YOU KNOW--
I'M SURE HE'D BE HAPPIER IN A BIGGER SPACE!
THERE'S NOTHING LEFT TO EXPLORE IN HIS FISH-BOWL!
WE COULD DIG A FISH-POND!
THAT WOULD BE COOL!
OK, LET'S DO IT!
LATER THAT DAY...
REX'S FISH-POND IS SO PRETTY!
GOOD JOB, PADDY!
THANKS, DAD, FOR BUYING SOME FRIENDS FOR REX!
REX'S A LITTLE LIKE ME--
HE JUST GOT FOUR SISTERS ALL AT ONCE!

38

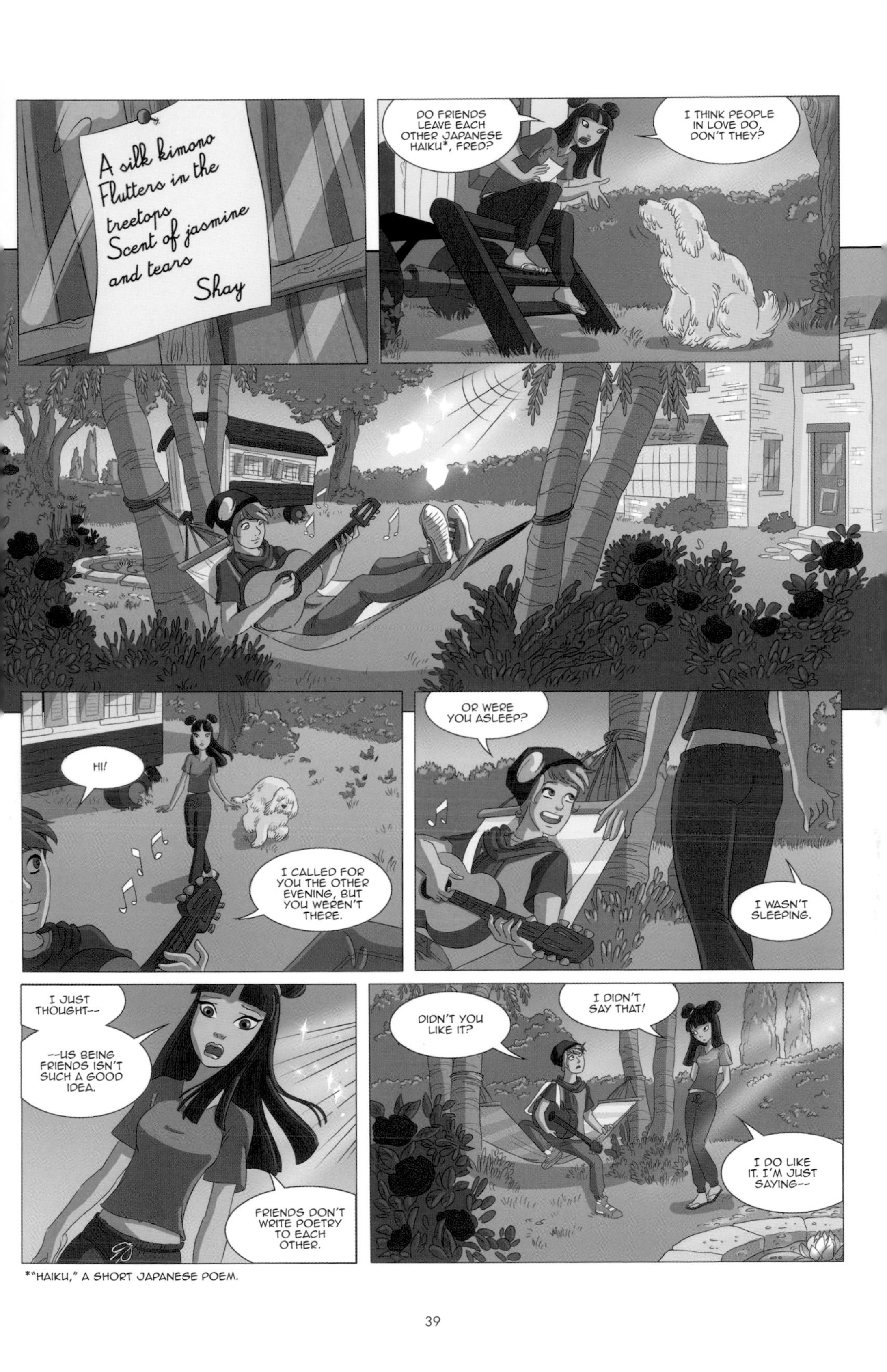
A silk kimono
Flutters in the
treetops
Scent of jasmine
and tears
Shay
DO FRIENDS LEAVE EACH OTHER JAPANESE HAIKU*, FRED?
I THINK PEOPLE IN LOVE DO, DON'T THEY?
HI!
I CALLED FOR YOU THE OTHER EVENING, BUT YOU WEREN'T THERE.
OR WERE YOU ASLEEP?
I WASN'T SLEEPING.
I JUST THOUGHT--
--US BEING FRIENDS ISN'T SUCH A GOOD IDEA.
FRIENDS DON'T WRITE POETRY TO EACH OTHER.
DIDN'T YOU LIKE IT?
I DIDN'T SAY THAT!
I DO LIKE IT. I'M JUST SAYING--

*"HAIKU," A SHORT JAPANESE POEM.

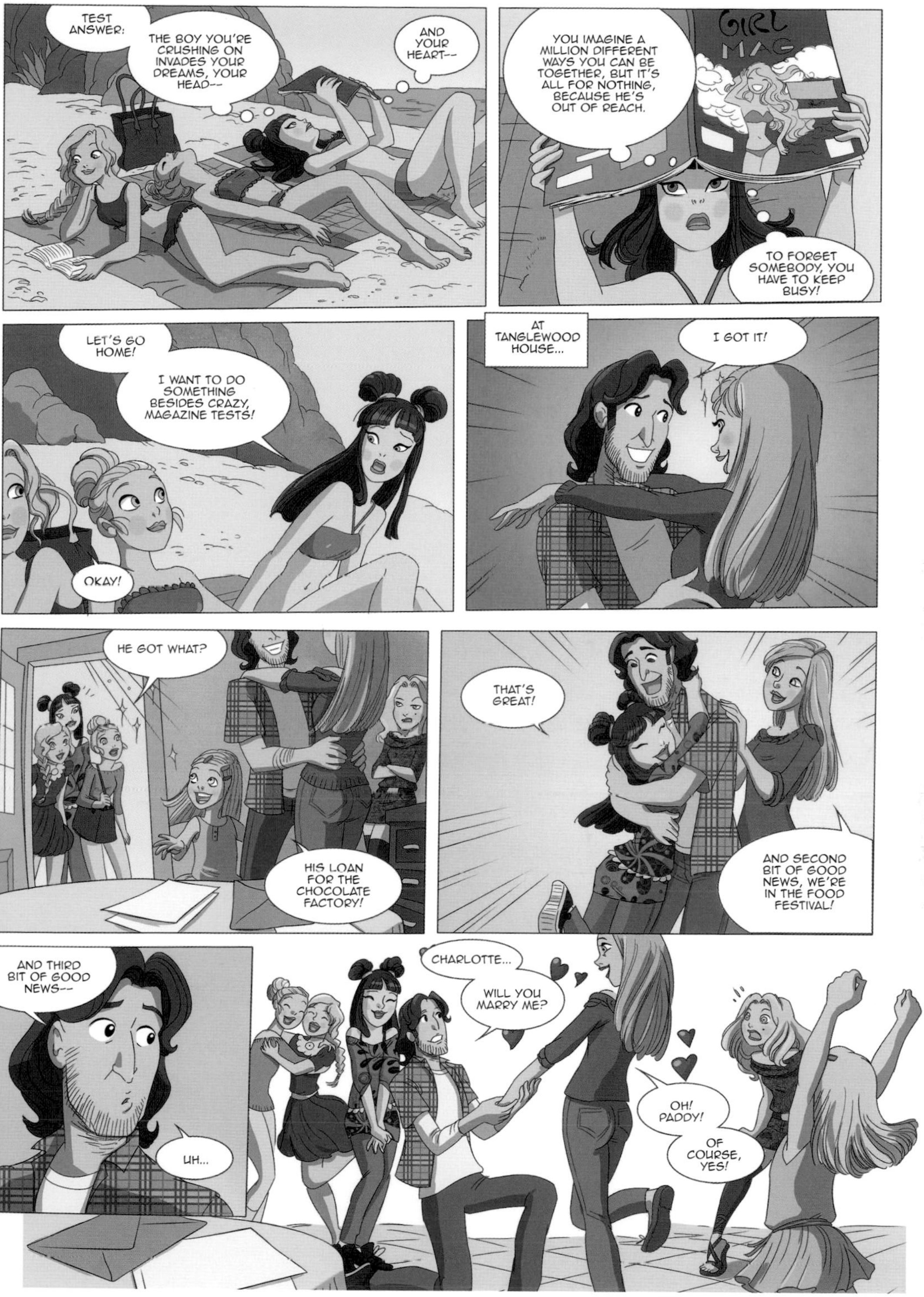
TEST ANSWER:
THE BOY YOU'RE CRUSHING ON INVADES YOUR DREAMS, YOUR HEAD--
AND YOUR HEART--
YOU IMAGINE A MILLION DIFFERENT WAYS YOU CAN BE TOGETHER, BUT IT'S ALL FOR NOTHING, BECAUSE HE'S OUT OF REACH.
GIRL MAG
TO FORGET SOMEBODY, YOU HAVE TO KEEP BUSY!
LET'S GO HOME!
I WANT TO DO SOMETHING BESIDES CRAZY, MAGAZINE TESTS!
OKAY!
AT TANGLEWOOD HOUSE...
I GOT IT!
HE GOT WHAT?
HIS LOAN FOR THE CHOCOLATE FACTORY!
THAT'S GREAT!
AND SECOND BIT OF GOOD NEWS, WE'RE IN THE FOOD FESTIVAL!
AND THIRD BIT OF GOOD NEWS--
UH...
CHARLOTTE...
WILL YOU MARRY ME?
OH! PADDY!
OF COURSE, YES!

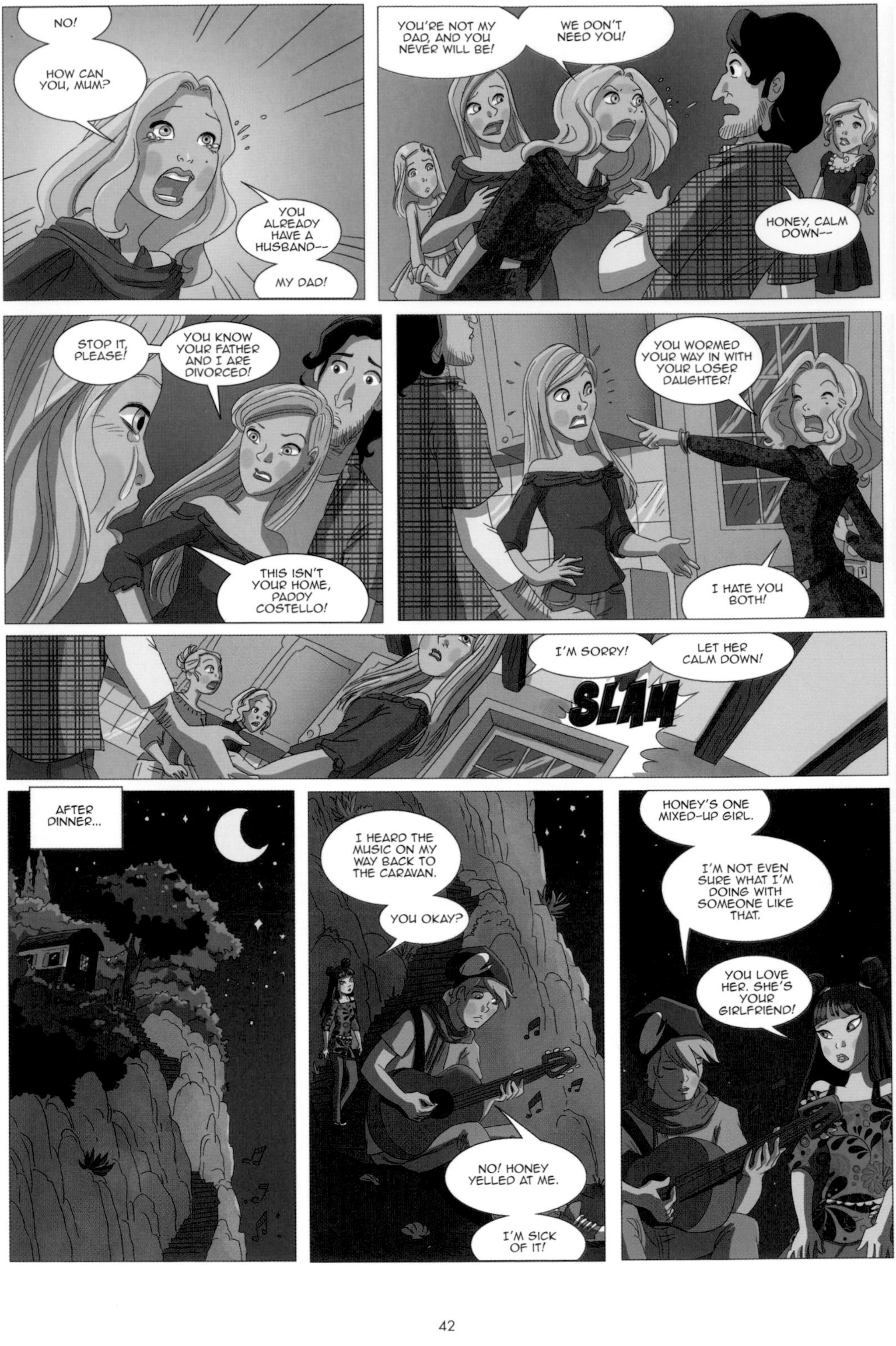
NO!
HOW CAN YOU, MUM?
YOU ALREADY HAVE A HUSBAND--
MY DAD!
YOU'RE NOT MY DAD, AND YOU NEVER WILL BE!
WE DON'T NEED YOU!
HONEY, CALM DOWN--
STOP IT, PLEASE!
YOU KNOW YOUR FATHER AND I ARE DIVORCED!
THIS ISN'T YOUR HOME, PADDY COSTELLO!
YOU WORMED YOUR WAY IN WITH YOUR LOSER DAUGHTER!
I HATE YOU BOTH!
I'M SORRY!
LET HER CALM DOWN!
SLAM
AFTER DINNER...
I HEARD THE MUSIC ON MY WAY BACK TO THE CARAVAN.
YOU OKAY?
NO! HONEY YELLED AT ME.
I'M SICK OF IT!
HONEY'S ONE MIXED-UP GIRL.
I'M NOT EVEN SURE WHAT I'M DOING WITH SOMEONE LIKE THAT.
YOU LOVE HER. SHE'S YOUR GIRLFRIEND!

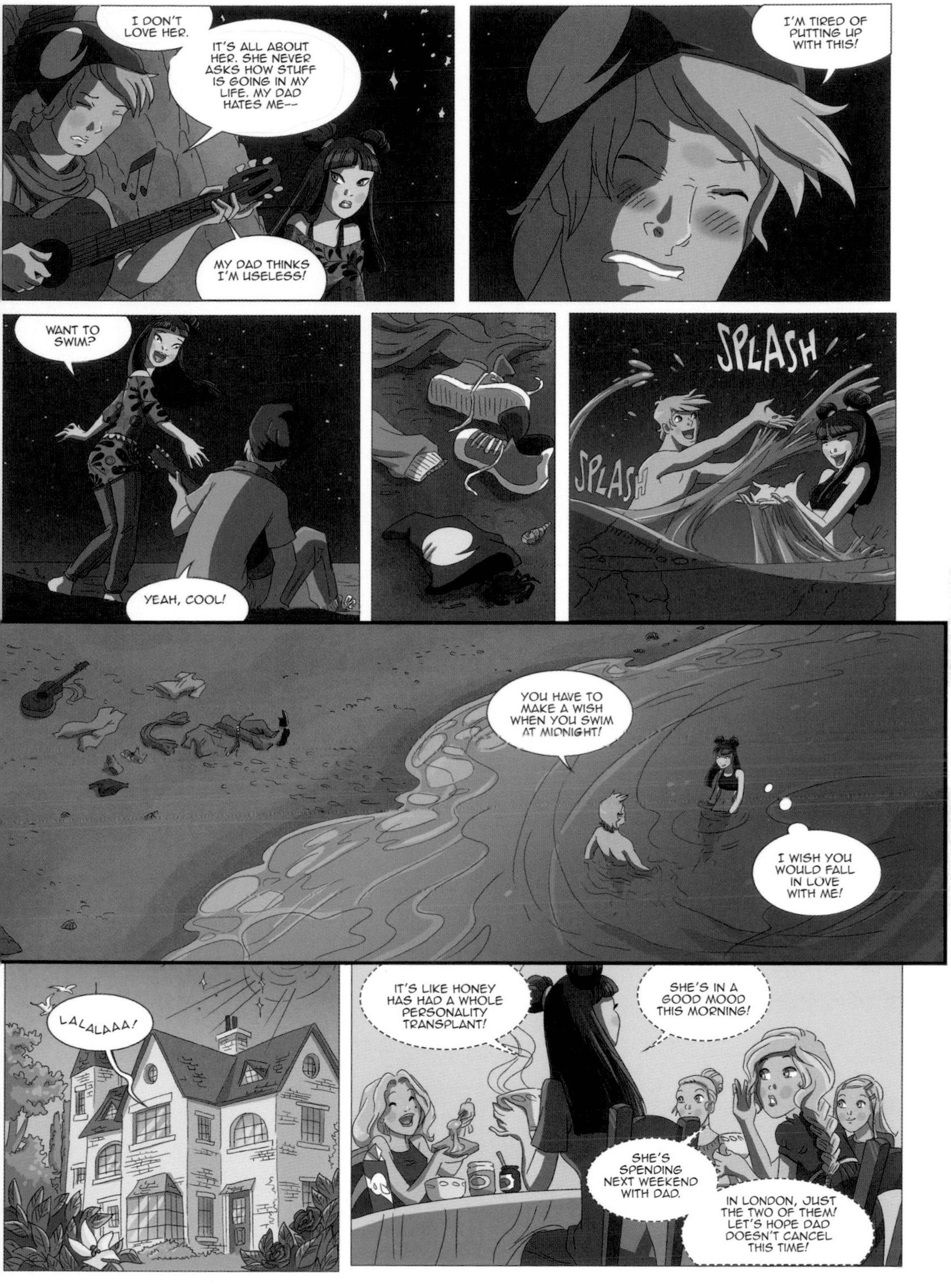
I DON'T LOVE HER.
IT'S ALL ABOUT HER. SHE NEVER ASKS HOW STUFF IS GOING IN MY LIFE. MY DAD HATES ME--
MY DAD THINKS I'M USELESS!
I'M TIRED OF PUTTING UP WITH THIS!
WANT TO SWIM?
YEAH, COOL!
SPLASH
SPLASH
YOU HAVE TO MAKE A WISH WHEN YOU SWIM AT MIDNIGHT!
I WISH YOU WOULD FALL IN LOVE WITH ME!
LALALAAA!
IT'S LIKE HONEY HAS HAD A WHOLE PERSONALITY TRANSPLANT!
SHE'S IN A GOOD MOOD THIS MORNING!
SHE'S SPENDING NEXT WEEKEND WITH DAD.
IN LONDON, JUST THE TWO OF THEM! LET'S HOPE DAD DOESN'T CANCEL THIS TIME!

45

Sweeties PART TWO "THE GYPSY GHOST"

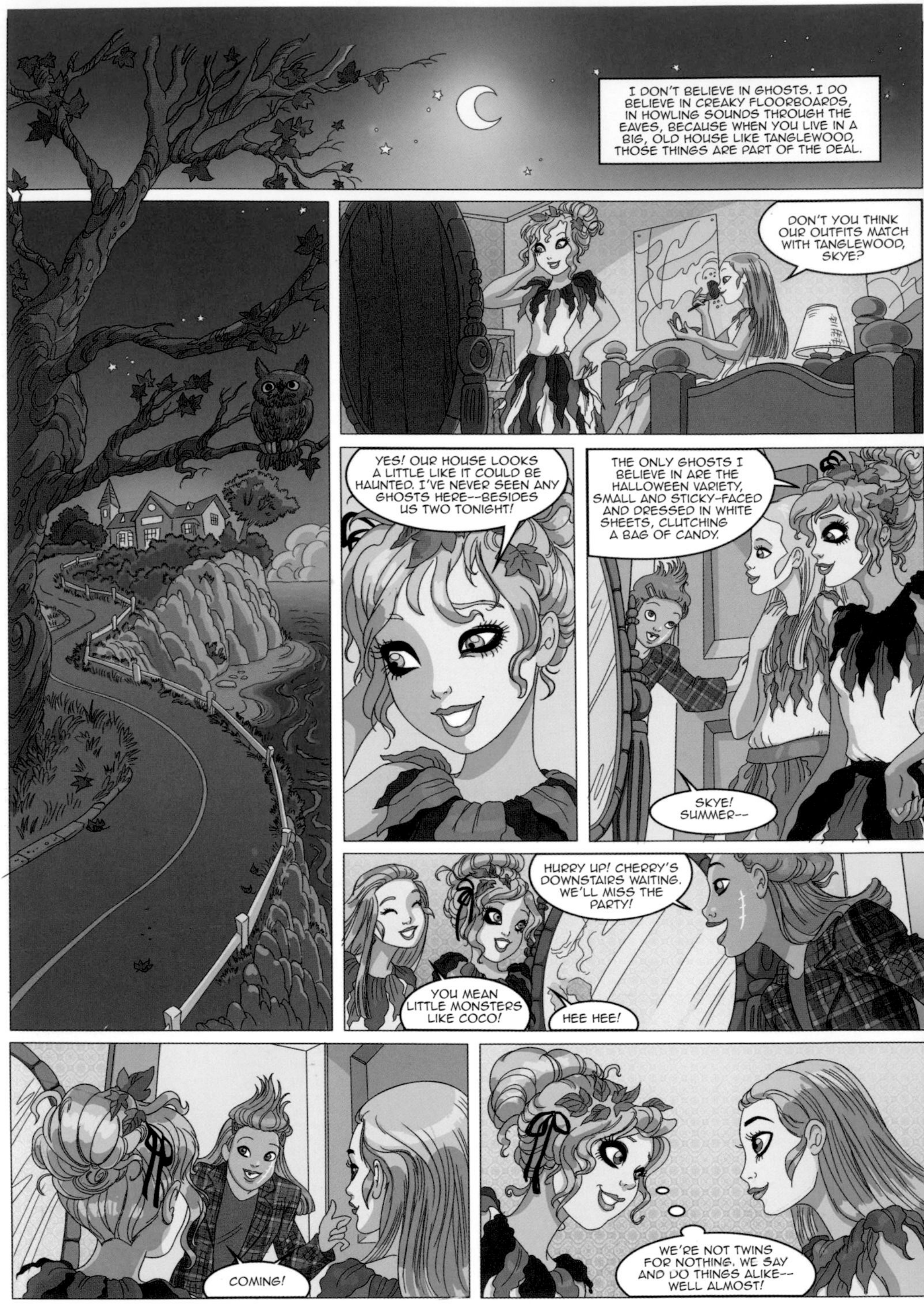
I DON'T BELIEVE IN GHOSTS. I DO BELIEVE IN CREAKY FLOORBOARDS, IN HOWLING SOUNDS THROUGH THE EAVES, BECAUSE WHEN YOU LIVE IN A BIG, OLD HOUSE LIKE TANGLEWOOD, THOSE THINGS ARE PART OF THE DEAL.
DON'T YOU THINK OUR OUTFITS MATCH WITH TANGLEWOOD, SKYE?
YES! OUR HOUSE LOOKS A LITTLE LIKE IT COULD BE HAUNTED. I'VE NEVER SEEN ANY GHOSTS HERE--BESIDES US TWO TONIGHT!
THE ONLY GHOSTS I BELIEVE IN ARE THE HALLOWEEN VARIETY, SMALL AND STICKY-FACED AND DRESSED IN WHITE SHEETS, CLUTCHING A BAG OF CANDY.
SKYE! SUMMER--
HURRY UP! CHERRY'S DOWNSTAIRS WAITING. WE'LL MISS THE PARTY!
YOU MEAN LITTLE MONSTERS LIKE COCO!
HEE HEE!
COMING!
WE'RE NOT TWINS FOR NOTHING. WE SAY AND DO THINGS ALIKE-- WELL ALMOST!

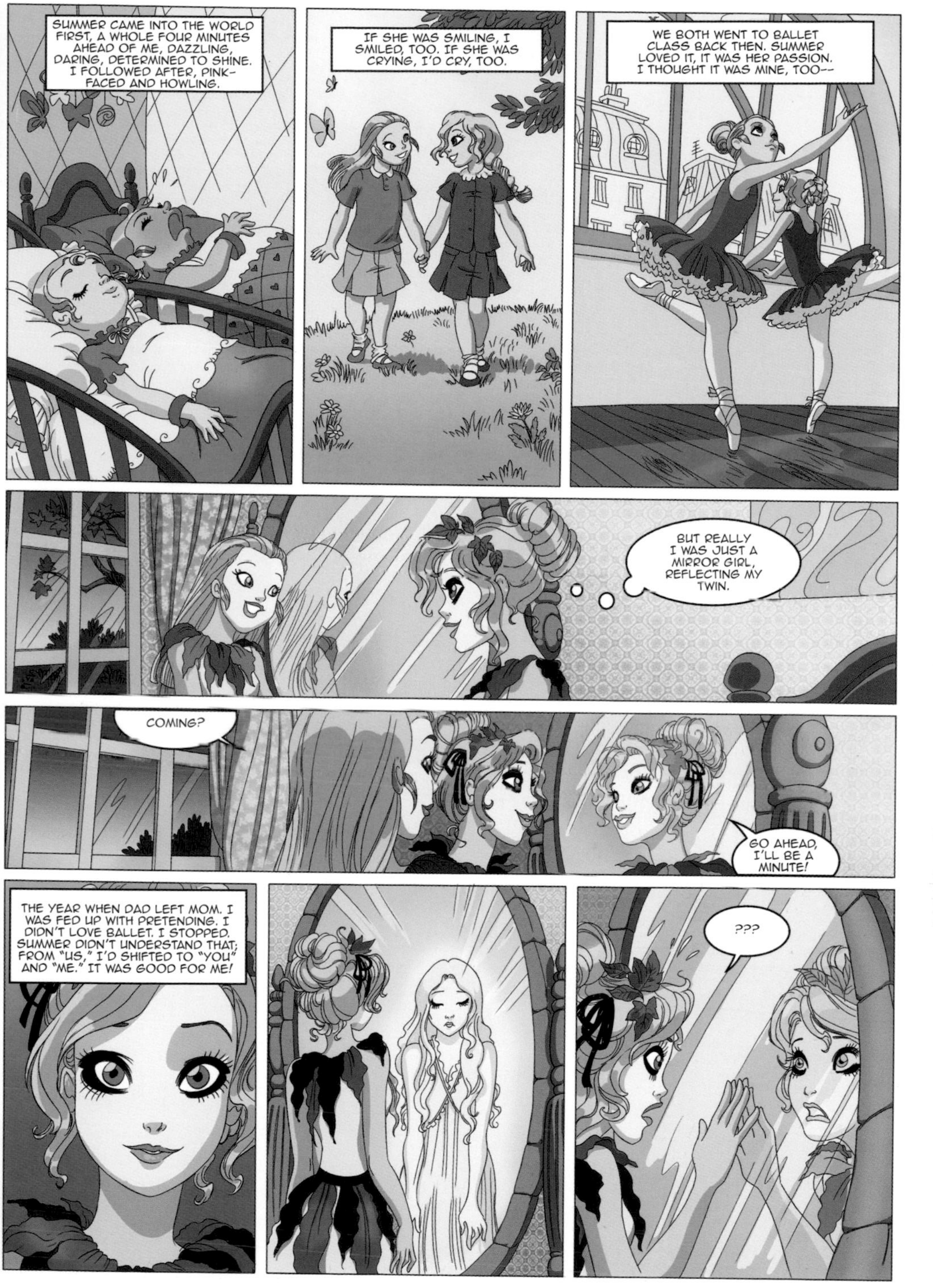
SUMMER CAME INTO THE WORLD FIRST, A WHOLE FOUR MINUTES AHEAD OF ME, DAZZLING, DARING, DETERMINED TO SHINE. I FOLLOWED AFTER, PINK-FACED AND HOWLING.
IF SHE WAS SMILING, I SMILED, TOO. IF SHE WAS CRYING, I'D CRY, TOO.
WE BOTH WENT TO BALLET CLASS BACK THEN. SUMMER LOVED IT, IT WAS HER PASSION. I THOUGHT IT WAS MINE, TOO--
BUT REALLY I WAS JUST A MIRROR GIRL, REFLECTING MY TWIN.
COMING?
GO AHEAD, I'LL BE A MINUTE!
THE YEAR WHEN DAD LEFT MOM. I WAS FED UP WITH PRETENDING. I DIDN'T LOVE BALLET. I STOPPED. SUMMER DIDN'T UNDERSTAND THAT; FROM "US," I'D SHIFTED TO "YOU" AND "ME." IT WAS GOOD FOR ME!
???

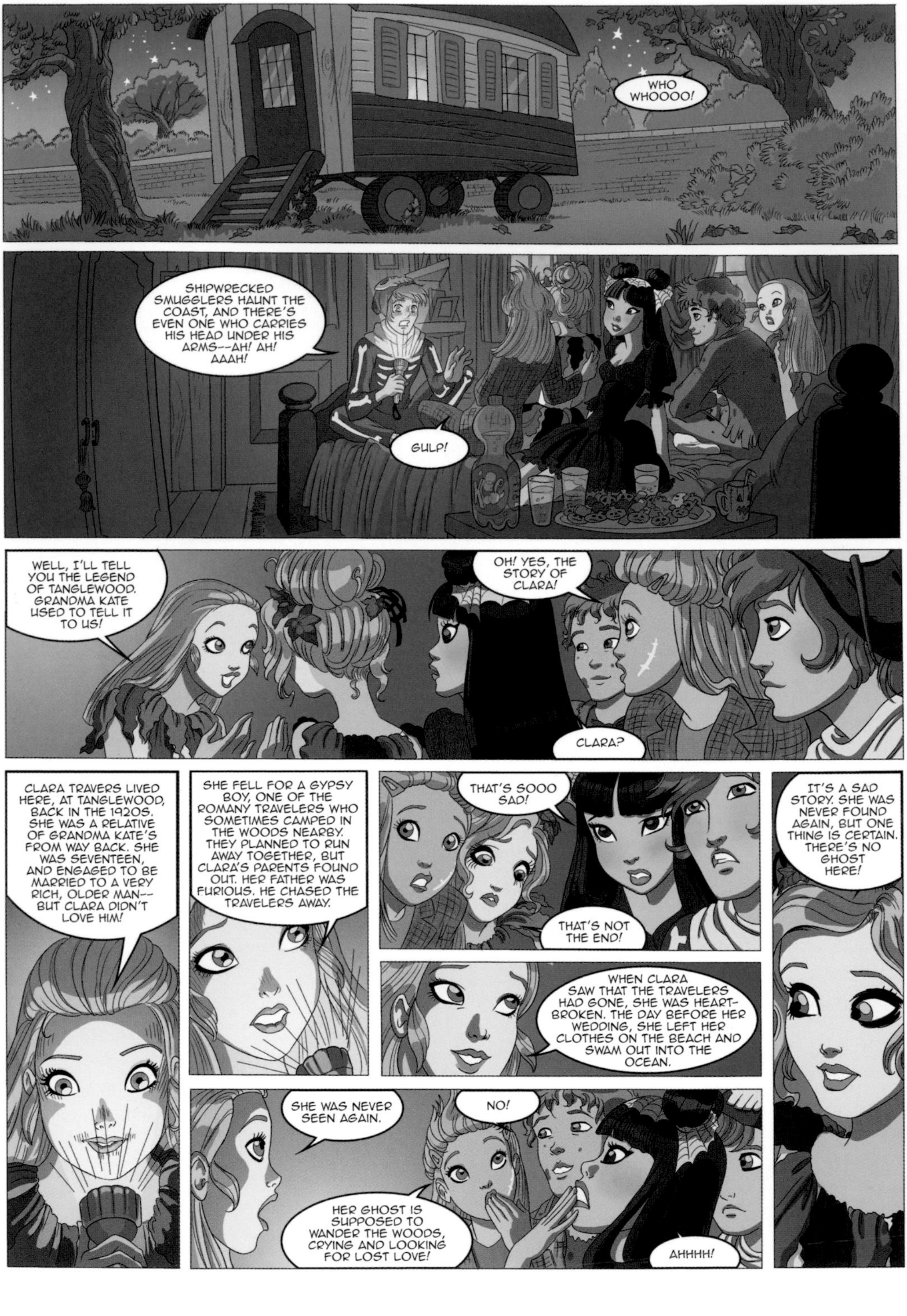
WHO WHOOOO!
SHIPWRECKED SMUGGLERS HAUNT THE COAST, AND THERE'S EVEN ONE WHO CARRIES HIS HEAD UNDER HIS ARMS--AH! AH! AAAH!
GULP!
WELL, I'LL TELL YOU THE LEGEND OF TANGLEWOOD. GRANDMA KATE USED TO TELL IT TO US!
OH! YES, THE STORY OF CLARA!
CLARA?
CLARA TRAVERS LIVED HERE, AT TANGLEWOOD, BACK IN THE 1920S. SHE WAS A RELATIVE OF GRANDMA KATE'S FROM WAY BACK. SHE WAS SEVENTEEN, AND ENGAGED TO BE MARRIED TO A VERY RICH, OLDER MAN--BUT CLARA DIDN'T LOVE HIM!
SHE FELL FOR A GYPSY BOY, ONE OF THE ROMANY TRAVELERS WHO SOMETIMES CAMPED IN THE WOODS NEARBY. THEY PLANNED TO RUN AWAY TOGETHER, BUT CLARA'S PARENTS FOUND OUT. HER FATHER WAS FURIOUS. HE CHASED THE TRAVELERS AWAY.
THAT'S SOOO SAD!
THAT'S NOT THE END!
WHEN CLARA SAW THAT THE TRAVELERS HAD GONE, SHE WAS HEART-BROKEN. THE DAY BEFORE HER WEDDING, SHE LEFT HER CLOTHES ON THE BEACH AND SWAM OUT INTO THE OCEAN.
SHE WAS NEVER SEEN AGAIN.
NO!
HER GHOST IS SUPPOSED TO WANDER THE WOODS, CRYING AND LOOKING FOR LOST LOVE!
AHHHH!
IT'S A SAD STORY. SHE WAS NEVER FOUND AGAIN, BUT ONE THING IS CERTAIN. THERE'S NO GHOST HERE!

THE NEXT MORNING.

WHAT'S ALL THIS?

DAD AND CHARLOTTE HAVE BEGUN TO CLEAR THE ATTIC FOR MY BEDROOM. IT'LL BE COLD IN THE WINTER IN THE CARAVAN!

I DON'T SUPPOSE YOU REMEMBER THAT OLD STORY YOUR GRAN USED TO TELL?

A SAD STORY ABOUT CLARA TRAVERS? I THINK THESE LETTERS BELONGED TO HER!

MOM, CAN I HAVE THAT BIRDCAGE?

AND ME, THE VIOLIN, PLEASE!

OK, THEN! SO LONG AS CHERRY AND SKYE PICK SOMETHING, TOO!

MOM, DO YOU THINK THESE CLOTHES BELONGED TO CLARA TRAVERS?

YES!

SUMMER, WILL YOU HELP ME CARRY CLARA'S TRUNK INTO THE BEDROOM?

THANKS, CHARLOTTE, BUT I DON'T LIKE OLD THINGS!

SKYE, YOU LOVE VINTAGE CLOTHES, DON'T YOU? I THINK CLARA WOULD HAVE WANTED YOU TO HAVE THEM! AND HONEY WON'T WANT THEM, SHE'S STILL POUTING IN HER BEDROOM!

WHO WANTS TO TASTE MY MARSH-MALLOW?

AH! NO-- MARSHMALLOW'S ANYTHING BUT BLAND! IT'S SWEET, LIGHT, LIKE A LITTLE BIT OF PARADISE!

I DON'T LIKE IT! IT'S BLAND!

YES, IF YOU WANT.

55

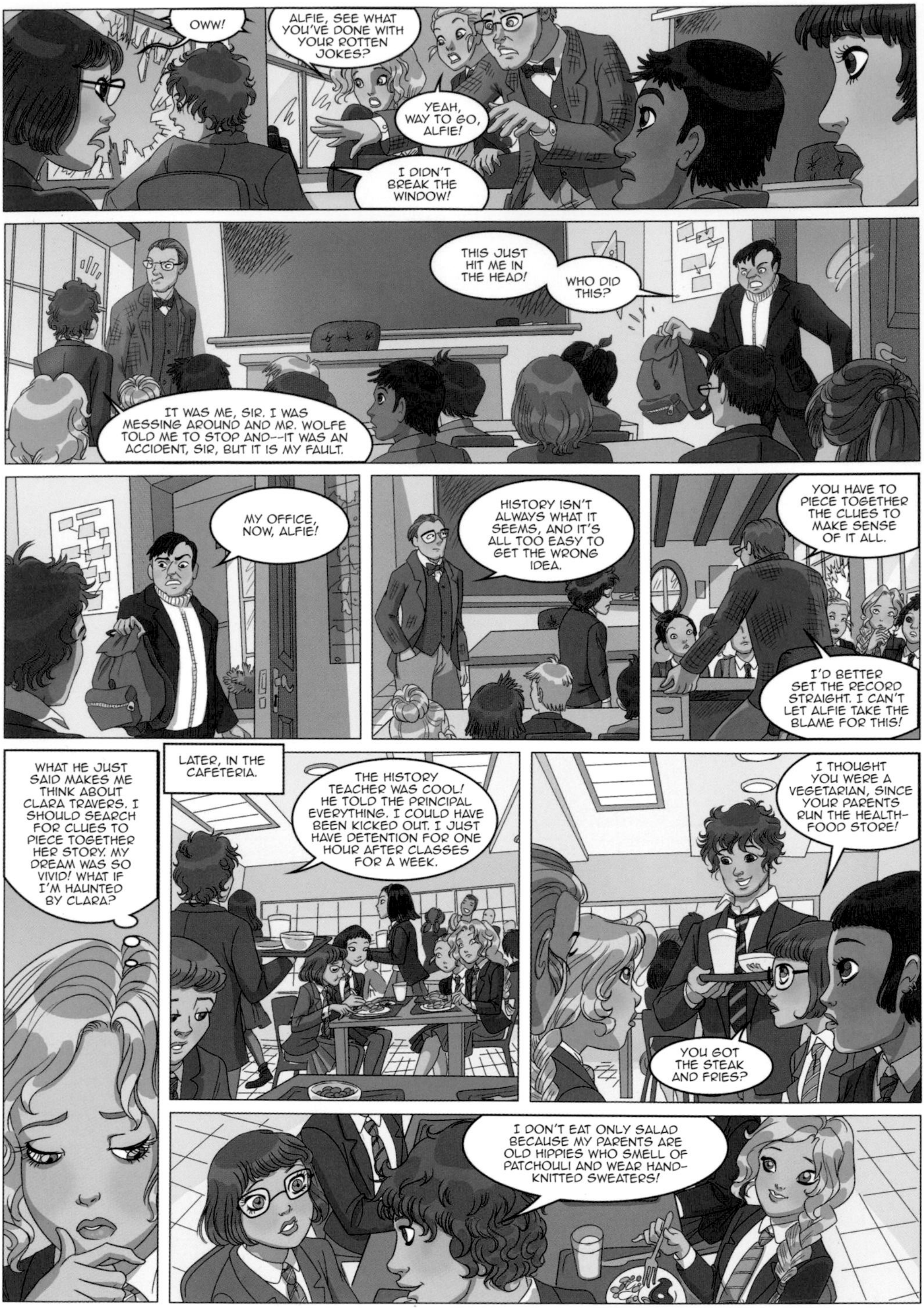
OWW!
ALFIE, SEE WHAT YOU'VE DONE WITH YOUR ROTTEN JOKES?
YEAH, WAY TO GO, ALFIE!
I DIDN'T BREAK THE WINDOW!
THIS JUST HIT ME IN THE HEAD!
WHO DID THIS?
IT WAS ME, SIR. I WAS MESSING AROUND AND MR. WOLFE TOLD ME TO STOP AND--IT WAS AN ACCIDENT, SIR, BUT IT IS MY FAULT.
MY OFFICE, NOW, ALFIE!
HISTORY ISN'T ALWAYS WHAT IT SEEMS, AND IT'S ALL TOO EASY TO GET THE WRONG IDEA.
YOU HAVE TO PIECE TOGETHER THE CLUES TO MAKE SENSE OF IT ALL.
I'D BETTER SET THE RECORD STRAIGHT. I CAN'T LET ALFIE TAKE THE BLAME FOR THIS!
WHAT HE JUST SAID MAKES ME THINK ABOUT CLARA TRAVERS. I SHOULD SEARCH FOR CLUES TO PIECE TOGETHER HER STORY. MY DREAM WAS SO VIVID! WHAT IF I'M HAUNTED BY CLARA?
LATER, IN THE CAFETERIA.
THE HISTORY TEACHER WAS COOL! HE TOLD THE PRINCIPAL EVERYTHING. I COULD HAVE BEEN KICKED OUT. I JUST HAVE DETENTION FOR ONE HOUR AFTER CLASSES FOR A WEEK.
I THOUGHT YOU WERE A VEGETARIAN, SINCE YOUR PARENTS RUN THE HEALTH-FOOD STORE!
YOU GOT THE STEAK AND FRIES?
I DON'T EAT ONLY SALAD BECAUSE MY PARENTS ARE OLD HIPPIES WHO SMELL OF PATCHOULI AND WEAR HAND-KNITTED SWEATERS!

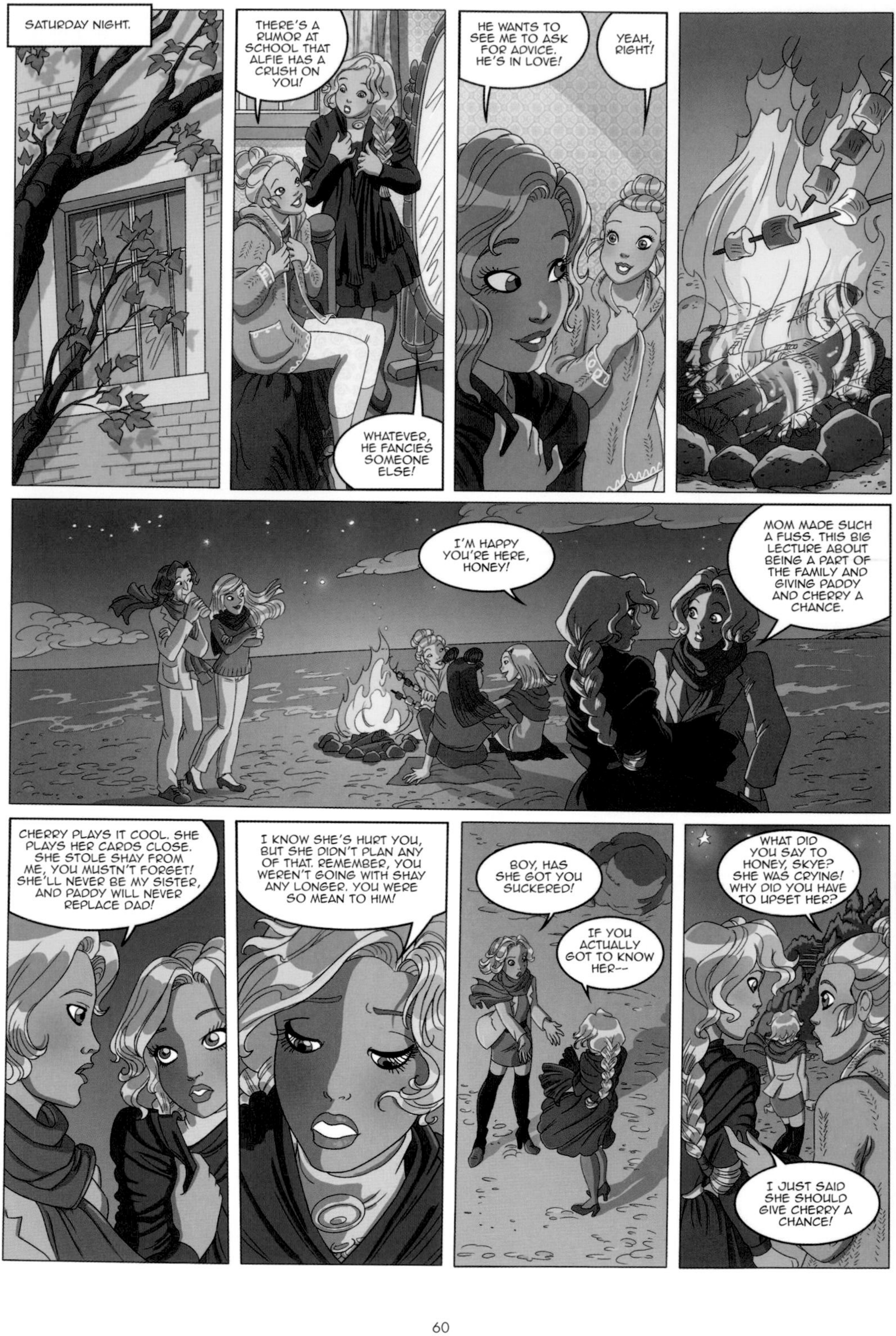
SATURDAY NIGHT.
THERE'S A RUMOR AT SCHOOL THAT ALFIE HAS A CRUSH ON YOU!
WHATEVER, HE FANCIES SOMEONE ELSE!
HE WANTS TO SEE ME TO ASK FOR ADVICE. HE'S IN LOVE!
YEAH, RIGHT!
I'M HAPPY YOU'RE HERE, HONEY!
MOM MADE SUCH A FUSS. THIS BIG LECTURE ABOUT BEING A PART OF THE FAMILY AND GIVING PADDY AND CHERRY A CHANCE.
CHERRY PLAYS IT COOL. SHE PLAYS HER CARDS CLOSE. SHE STOLE SHAY FROM ME, YOU MUSTN'T FORGET! SHE'LL NEVER BE MY SISTER, AND PADDY WILL NEVER REPLACE DAD!
I KNOW SHE'S HURT YOU, BUT SHE DIDN'T PLAN ANY OF THAT. REMEMBER, YOU WEREN'T GOING WITH SHAY ANY LONGER. YOU WERE SO MEAN TO HIM!
BOY, HAS SHE GOT YOU SUCKERED!
IF YOU ACTUALLY GOT TO KNOW HER--
WHAT DID YOU SAY TO HONEY, SKYE? SHE WAS CRYING! WHY DID YOU HAVE TO UPSET HER?
I JUST SAID SHE SHOULD GIVE CHERRY A CHANCE!

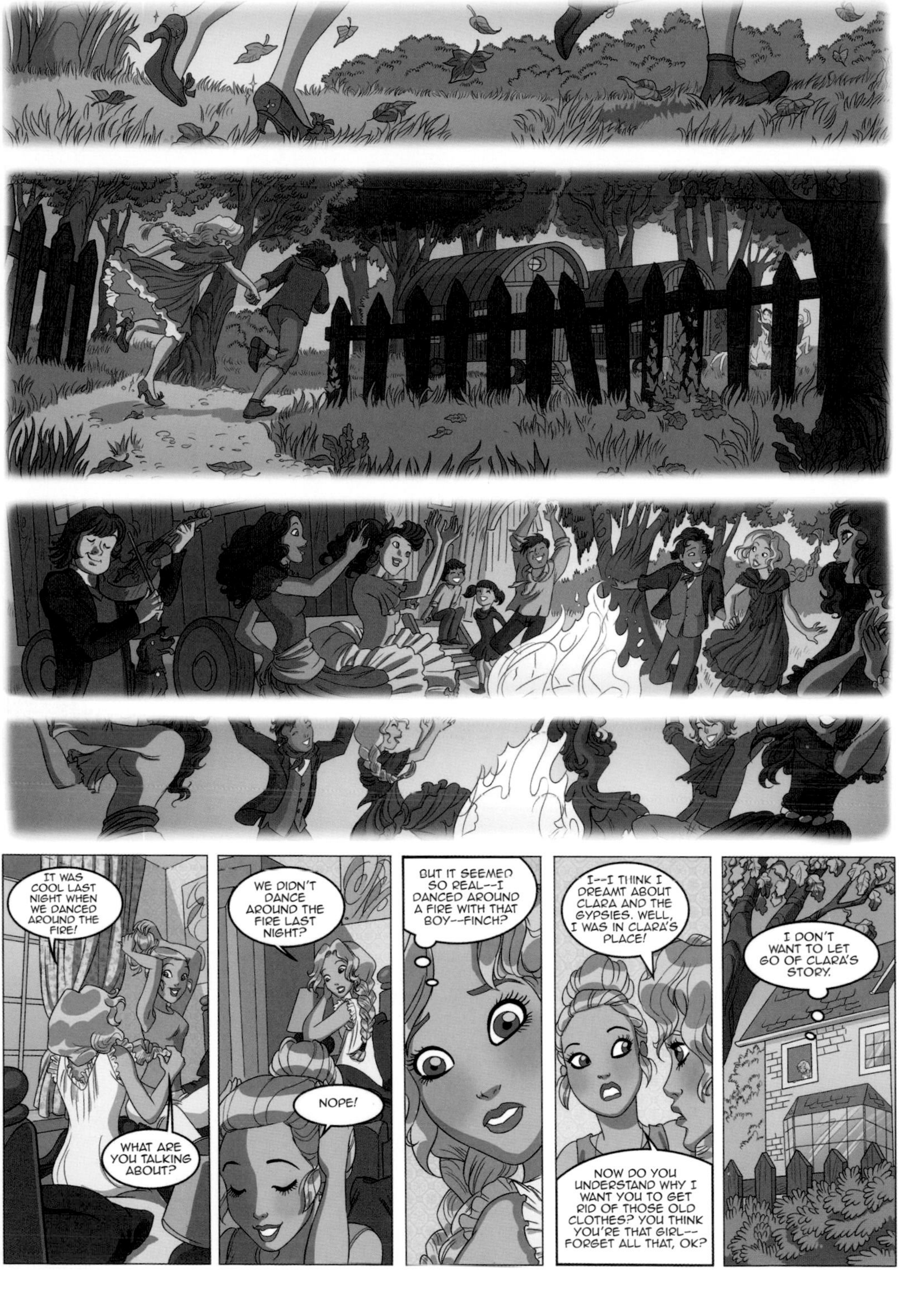
IT WAS COOL LAST NIGHT WHEN WE DANCED AROUND THE FIRE!
WHAT ARE YOU TALKING ABOUT?
WE DIDN'T DANCE AROUND THE FIRE LAST NIGHT?
NOPE!
BUT IT SEEMED SO REAL--I DANCED AROUND A FIRE WITH THAT BOY--FINCH?
I--I THINK I DREAMT ABOUT CLARA AND THE GYPSIES. WELL, I WAS IN CLARA'S PLACE!
NOW DO YOU UNDERSTAND WHY I WANT YOU TO GET RID OF THOSE OLD CLOTHES? YOU THINK YOU'RE THAT GIRL--FORGET ALL THAT, OK?
I DON'T WANT TO LET GO OF CLARA'S STORY.

The Mad Hatter
SATURDAY AFTERNOON.
OK, SKYE, I NEED YOUR HELP!
YOU'RE A GIRL, SO YOU MIGHT BE ABLE TO TELL ME WHERE I'M GOING WRONG. I HAVE A PLAN, AND YOU CAN HELP ME MAKE IT HAPPEN. THE THING IS--I WANT TO BE IRRESISTIBLE TO WOMEN!
PFFFFFFF!
WHAT? IS THAT FUNNY OR SOMETHING?
NO, NO, I WASN'T LAUGHING. IT'S JUST SOMETHING WENT DOWN THE WRONG WAY.
YEAH, RIGHT. THAT'S EXACTLY THE PROBLEM. I'VE LIKED THIS GIRL FOR A WHILE, BUT SHE THINKS I'M AN IDIOT. I'M TIRED OF IT!
GIRLS ARE A BIT OF A MYSTERY TO ME. I'D LIKE TO LEARN A LITTLE MORE ABOUT WHAT MAKES THEM HAPPY.
OK, I'LL GIVE YOU SOME FRIENDLY ADVICE!
OK, FIRST, WHAT'S OFF WITH ME?
YOU'RE TAKING NOTES? SERIOUSLY?

64

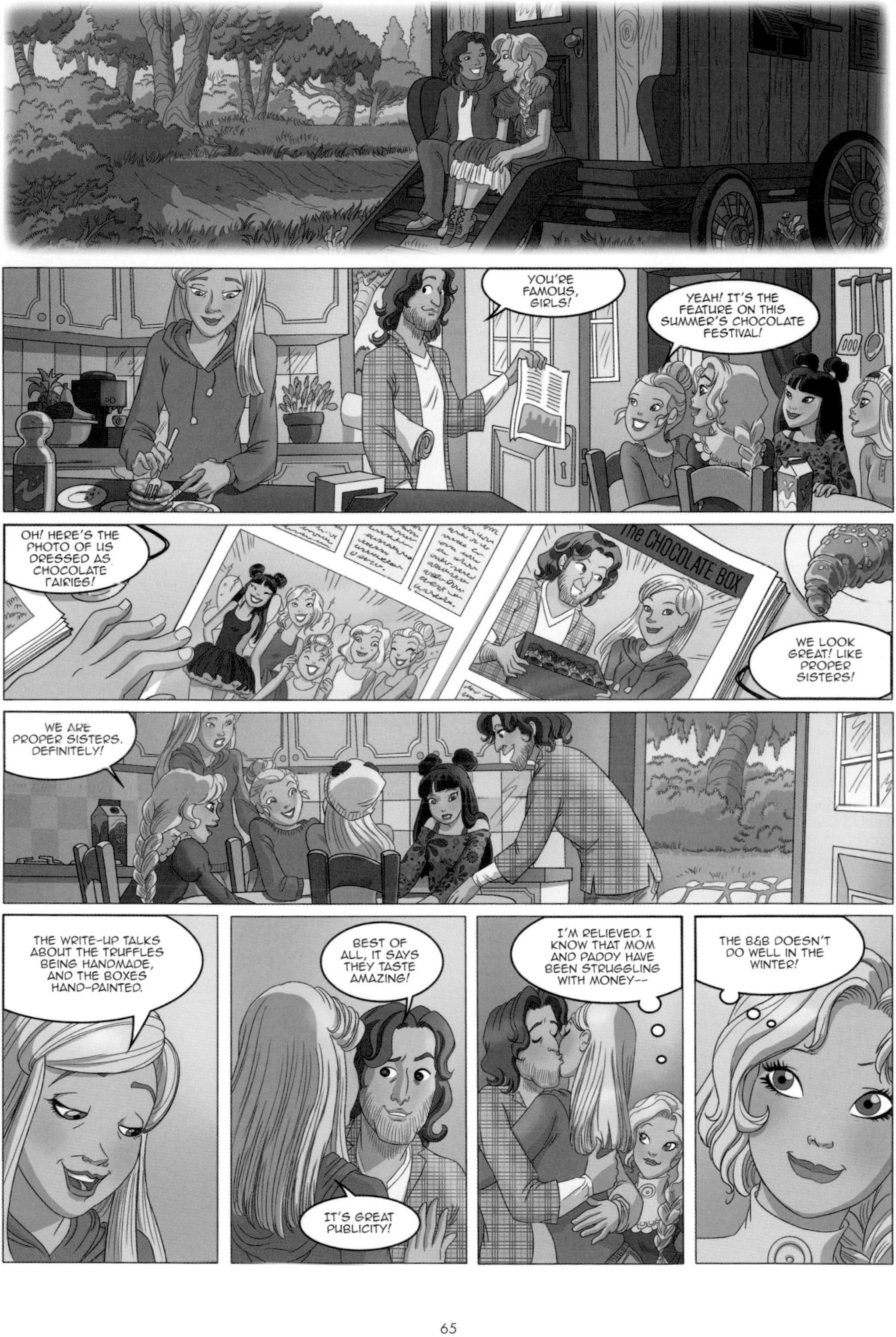
YOU'RE FAMOUS, GIRLS!
YEAH! IT'S THE FEATURE ON THIS SUMMER'S CHOCOLATE FESTIVAL!
OH! HERE'S THE PHOTO OF US DRESSED AS CHOCOLATE FAIRIES!
The CHOCOLATE BOX
WE LOOK GREAT! LIKE PROPER SISTERS!
WE ARE PROPER SISTERS. DEFINITELY!
THE WRITE-UP TALKS ABOUT THE TRUFFLES BEING HANDMADE, AND THE BOXES HAND-PAINTED.
BEST OF ALL, IT SAYS THEY TASTE AMAZING!
IT'S GREAT PUBLICITY!
I'M RELIEVED. I KNOW THAT MOM AND PADDY HAVE BEEN STRUGGLING WITH MONEY--
THE B&B DOESN'T DO WELL IN THE WINTER!

HEY HO! SKYE-- WAKE UP! YOU DIDN'T HEAR THE ALARM?

HUH? WHAT?

SUMMER, YOU KNOW THOSE OLD LETTERS FROM THE TRUNK? HAVE YOU SEEN THEM AT ALL?

WHAT LETTERS?

YOU KNOW-- THE BUNDLE OF CLARA TRAVERS' LETTERS. I CAN'T FIND THEM!

LOOK, I DON'T KNOW WHERE THEY ARE! I DIDN'T TOUCH THEM! WHY WOULD I BE INTERESTED IN SPOOKY, OLD LETTERS?

I'M NOT BLAMING YOU, SUMMER, IT'S JUST BUGGING ME THAT I'VE LOST THEM!

KEEPING MY DREAMS ALL TO MYSELF, IT'S SO HARD COMING BACK TO REALITY!

LATER, IN THE KITCHEN.

AFTER SCHOOL, GIRLS, COME GIVE US A HAND TO FILL THE CHOCOLATE BOXES. THANKS TO THE ARTICLE, ORDERS ARE NON-STOP!

CERTAINLY NOT! THAT'S SLAVERY!

HONEY, YOU'RE GETTING MORE AND MORE UNPLEASANT!

WHAT MOM SAYS IS TRUE. YOU NEVER USED TO BE LIKE THIS. I USED TO LOOK UP TO YOU. I THOUGHT YOU WERE THE COOLEST BIG SISTER IN THE WORLD--

BUT I WAS WRONG. YOU'RE NOT COOL AT ALL--YOU'RE SHALLOW AND SPITEFUL AND CRUEL!

67

WHAT DID YOU HAVE TO GO AND SAY THAT FOR?

IT'S JUST-- SHE NEVER HELPS. SHE'S NEVER HERE.

MAYBE YOU ACTUALLY GOT THROUGH TO HER? I'M NOT GETTING THINGS RIGHT WITH HONEY. PERHAPS WE NEED TO TAKE A HARDER LINE--FOR HER OWN SAKE.

MORE CHOCOLATE ORDERS? WOW!

WHO CAN GO BY THE POST OFFICE AFTER SCHOOL? TO SEND THESE THREE BOXES?

I CAN'T. I HAVE DANCE CLASS.

I'LL DO IT!

LATER THAT AFTERNOON.

AFTER WHAT I SAID TO HONEY THIS MORNING, I THINK SUMMER'S MAD AT ME!

POST OFFICE

SKYE, I'M SENSING A SADNESS ABOUT YOU TODAY!

YOU KNOW, I HAVE A GIFT. MY MOTHER WAS HALF-GYPSY AND SHE GAVE ME THE GIFT OF READING PALMS. GIVE ME YOUR HAND!

HELLO, MRS. LEE. YES, I'M NOT IN A GREAT MOOD.

I SEE ROMANCE! A BOY!

I'M NOT ALL THAT INTERESTED IN BOYS, REALLY!

I SEE--HE'S WEARING A RED SCARF!

DID SHE SEE FINCH?

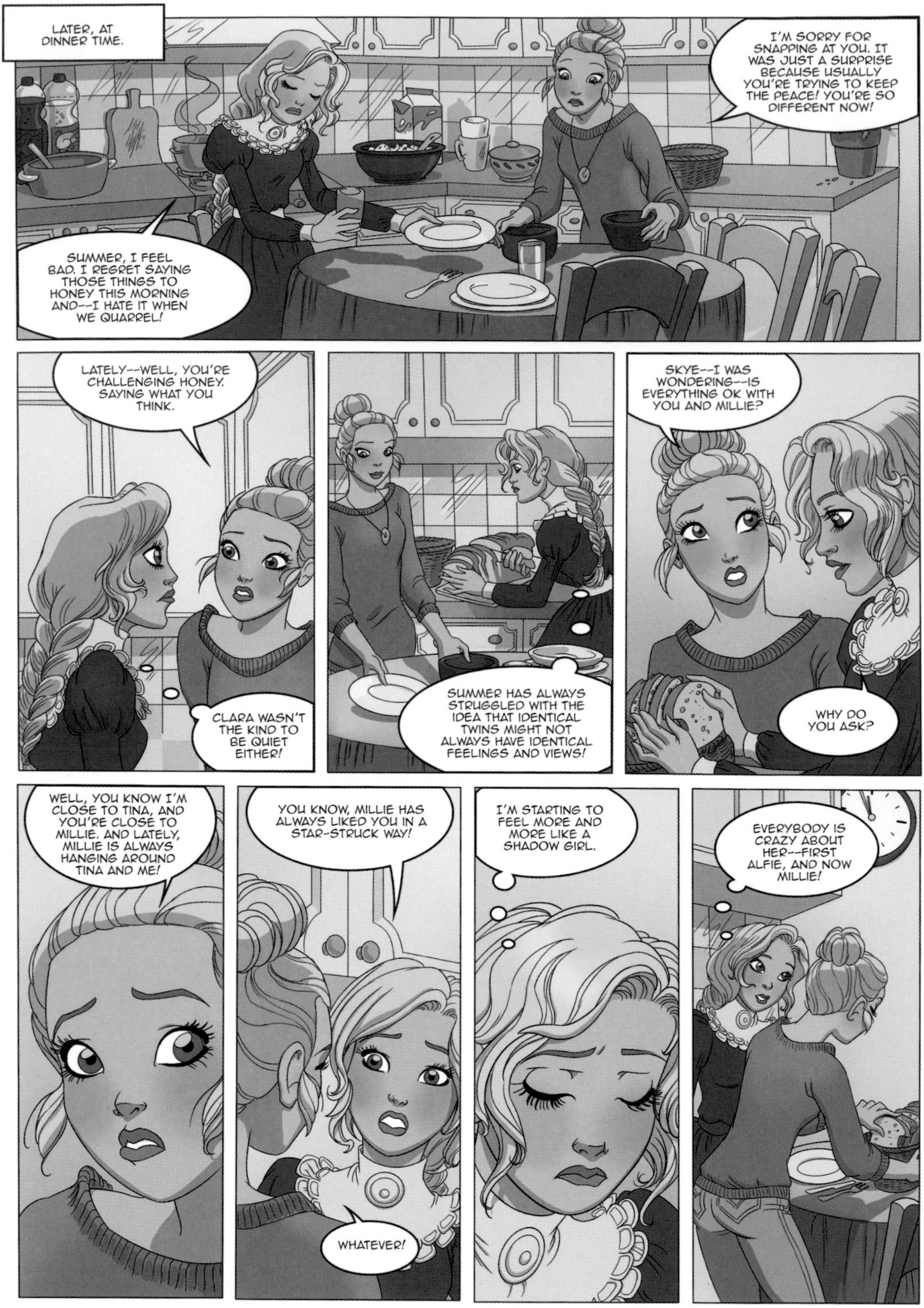
LATER, AT DINNER TIME.
I'M SORRY FOR SNAPPING AT YOU. IT WAS JUST A SURPRISE BECAUSE USUALLY YOU'RE TRYING TO KEEP THE PEACE! YOU'RE SO DIFFERENT NOW!
SUMMER, I FEEL BAD. I REGRET SAYING THOSE THINGS TO HONEY THIS MORNING AND--I HATE IT WHEN WE QUARREL!
LATELY--WELL, YOU'RE CHALLENGING HONEY. SAYING WHAT YOU THINK.
CLARA WASN'T THE KIND TO BE QUIET EITHER!
SUMMER HAS ALWAYS STRUGGLED WITH THE IDEA THAT IDENTICAL TWINS MIGHT NOT ALWAYS HAVE IDENTICAL FEELINGS AND VIEWS!
SKYE--I WAS WONDERING--IS EVERYTHING OK WITH YOU AND MILLIE?
WHY DO YOU ASK?
WELL, YOU KNOW I'M CLOSE TO TINA, AND YOU'RE CLOSE TO MILLIE. AND LATELY, MILLIE IS ALWAYS HANGING AROUND TINA AND ME!
YOU KNOW, MILLIE HAS ALWAYS LIKED YOU IN A STAR-STRUCK WAY!
WHATEVER!
I'M STARTING TO FEEL MORE AND MORE LIKE A SHADOW GIRL.
EVERYBODY IS CRAZY ABOUT HER--FIRST ALFIE, AND NOW MILLIE!

72

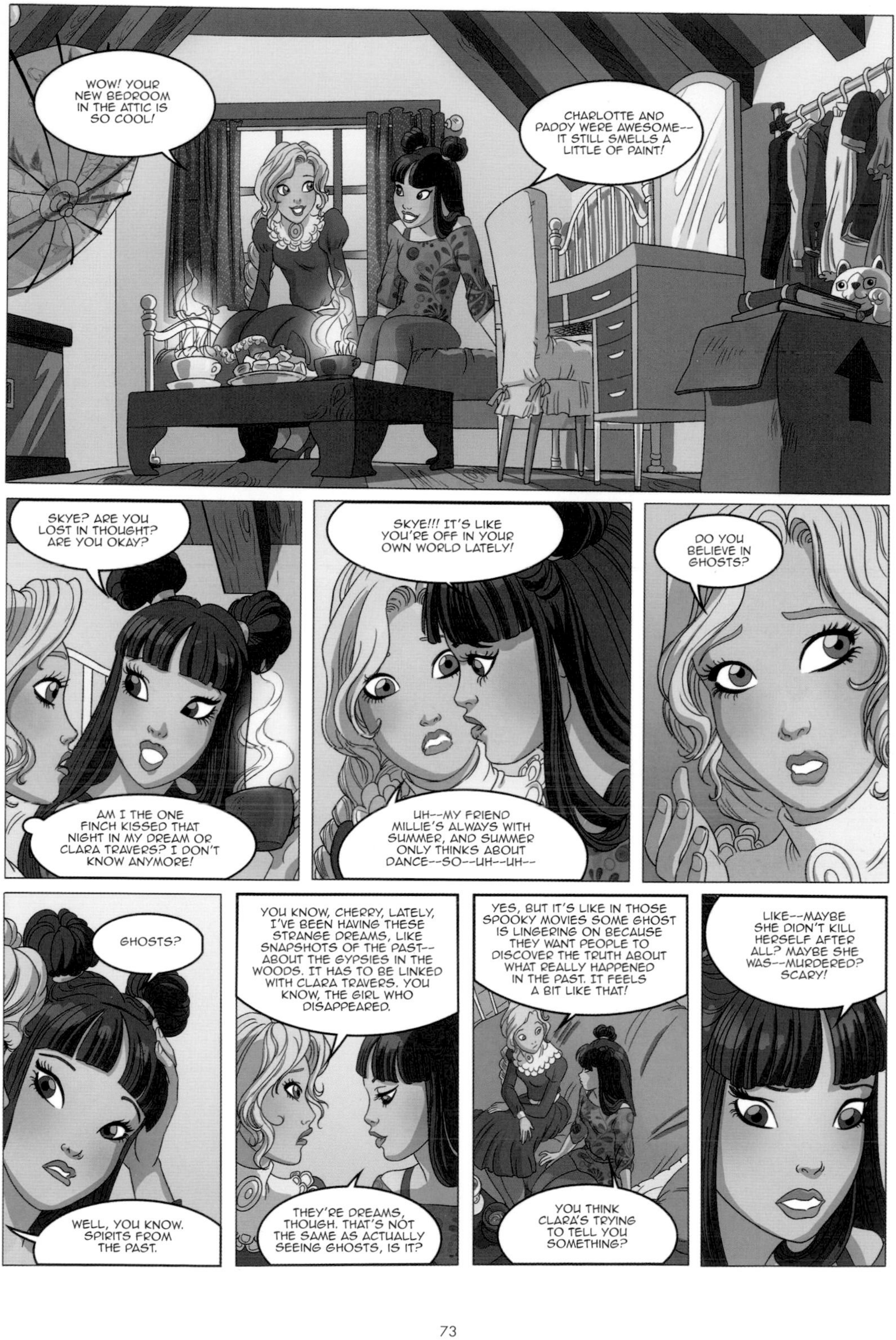
WOW! YOUR NEW BEDROOM IN THE ATTIC IS SO COOL!
CHARLOTTE AND PADDY WERE AWESOME-- IT STILL SMELLS A LITTLE OF PAINT!
SKYE? ARE YOU LOST IN THOUGHT? ARE YOU OKAY?
AM I THE ONE FINCH KISSED THAT NIGHT IN MY DREAM OR CLARA TRAVERS? I DON'T KNOW ANYMORE!
SKYE!!! IT'S LIKE YOU'RE OFF IN YOUR OWN WORLD LATELY!
UH--MY FRIEND MILLIE'S ALWAYS WITH SUMMER, AND SUMMER ONLY THINKS ABOUT DANCE--SO--UH--UH--
DO YOU BELIEVE IN GHOSTS?
GHOSTS?
WELL, YOU KNOW. SPIRITS FROM THE PAST.
YOU KNOW, CHERRY, LATELY, I'VE BEEN HAVING THESE STRANGE DREAMS, LIKE SNAPSHOTS OF THE PAST-- ABOUT THE GYPSIES IN THE WOODS. IT HAS TO BE LINKED WITH CLARA TRAVERS. YOU KNOW, THE GIRL WHO DISAPPEARED.
THEY'RE DREAMS, THOUGH. THAT'S NOT THE SAME AS ACTUALLY SEEING GHOSTS, IS IT?
YES, BUT IT'S LIKE IN THOSE SPOOKY MOVIES SOME GHOST IS LINGERING ON BECAUSE THEY WANT PEOPLE TO DISCOVER THE TRUTH ABOUT WHAT REALLY HAPPENED IN THE PAST. IT FEELS A BIT LIKE THAT!
YOU THINK CLARA'S TRYING TO TELL YOU SOMETHING?
LIKE--MAYBE SHE DIDN'T KILL HERSELF AFTER ALL? MAYBE SHE WAS--MURDERED? SCARY!

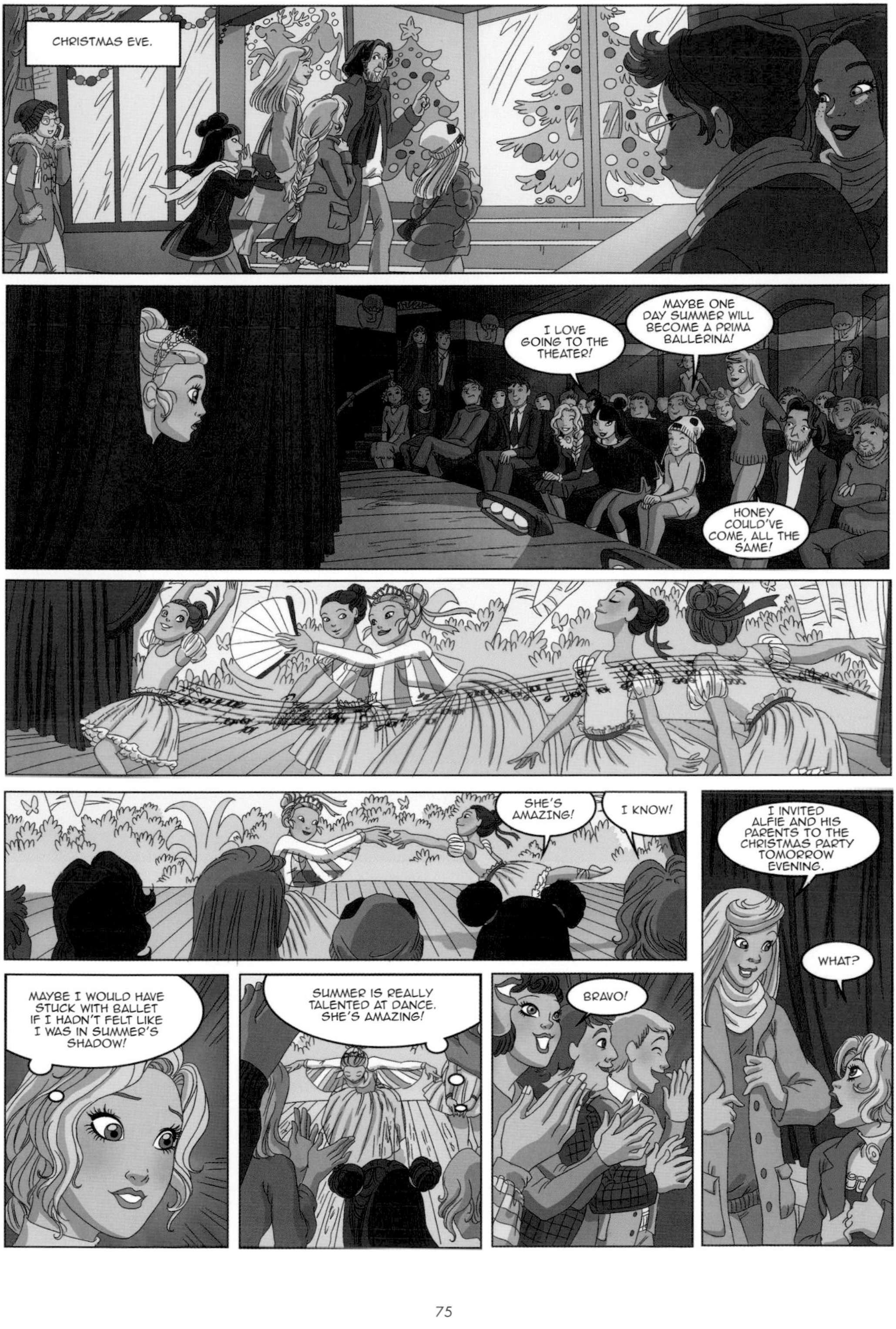
CHRISTMAS EVE.
I LOVE GOING TO THE THEATER!
MAYBE ONE DAY SUMMER WILL BECOME A PRIMA BALLERINA!
HONEY COULD'VE COME, ALL THE SAME!
SHE'S AMAZING!
I KNOW!
I INVITED ALFIE AND HIS PARENTS TO THE CHRISTMAS PARTY TOMORROW EVENING.
WHAT?
MAYBE I WOULD HAVE STUCK WITH BALLET IF I HADN'T FELT LIKE I WAS IN SUMMER'S SHADOW!
SUMMER IS REALLY TALENTED AT DANCE. SHE'S AMAZING!
BRAVO!

A LITTLE LATER.

COCO, PADDY CLEANED OUT THE OLD SHED IN THE YARD. THAT'LL MAKE A LITTLE HOUSE FOR YOUR LAMB!

DAD'S ON SKYPE TO WISH US A HAPPY CHRISTMAS!

I'LL CALL IT "MERRY CHRISTMAS"!

MERRY CHRISTMAS, DAD!

YOU'RE LOOKING SO GROWN UP!

IT'S EVENING NOW--THE WEATHER IS FANTASTIC! YOU'LL HAVE TO COME OUT AND VISIT!

WHAT TIME IS IT IN AUSTRALIA?

I'D LOVE TO SEE AUSTRALIA, IT HAS TO BE BETTER THAN THIS DUMP. WHEN WOULD BE A GOOD TIME?

BETTER WAIT UNTIL WE'VE SETTLED IN A BIT! GIVE YOUR MOM A CHANCE TO SAVE UP THE AIRFARES! GIRLS, IT'S BEEN GREAT TALKING TO YOU! BYE!

HE HAS A GIRLFRIEND, I'M SURE OF IT! HE SAID "WE."

NO WAY, HE WOULDN'T!

IF MOM HAS TO PAY FOR THE PLANE TICKETS, WE WON'T GO SEE HIM ANY TIME SOON!

HE DIDN'T EVEN FIND TIME TO SEND US A CHRISTMAS PRESENT-- EVEN THOUGH WE SENT HIM ONE!

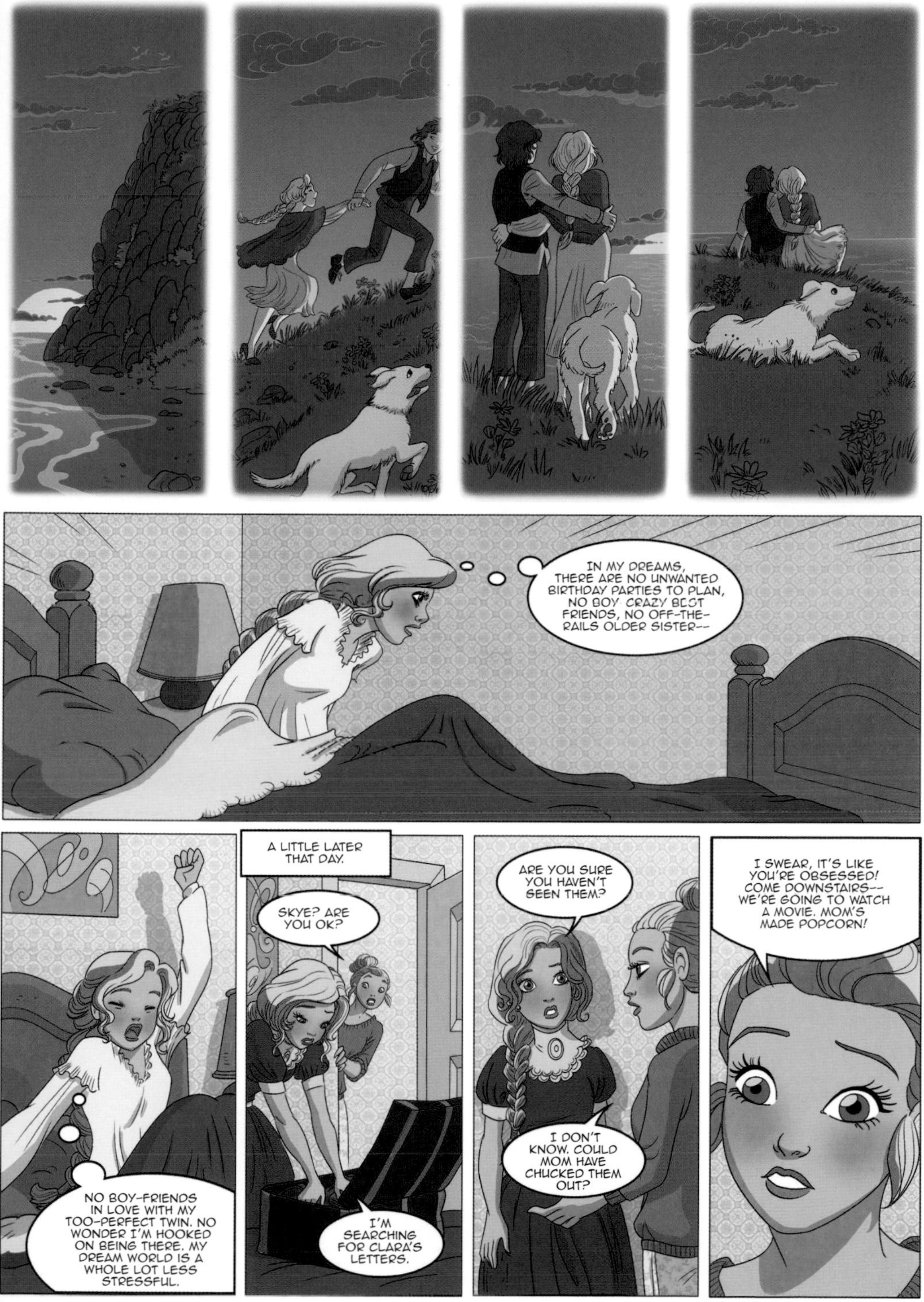
IN MY DREAMS, THERE ARE NO UNWANTED BIRTHDAY PARTIES TO PLAN, NO BOY CRAZY BEST FRIENDS, NO OFF-THE-RAILS OLDER SISTER--
NO BOY-FRIENDS IN LOVE WITH MY TOO-PERFECT TWIN. NO WONDER I'M HOOKED ON BEING THERE. MY DREAM WORLD IS A WHOLE LOT LESS STRESSFUL.
A LITTLE LATER THAT DAY.
SKYE? ARE YOU OK?
I'M SEARCHING FOR CLARA'S LETTERS.
ARE YOU SURE YOU HAVEN'T SEEN THEM?
I DON'T KNOW. COULD MOM HAVE CHUCKED THEM OUT?
I SWEAR, IT'S LIKE YOU'RE OBSESSED! COME DOWNSTAIRS-- WE'RE GOING TO WATCH A MOVIE. MOM'S MADE POPCORN!

83

84

85

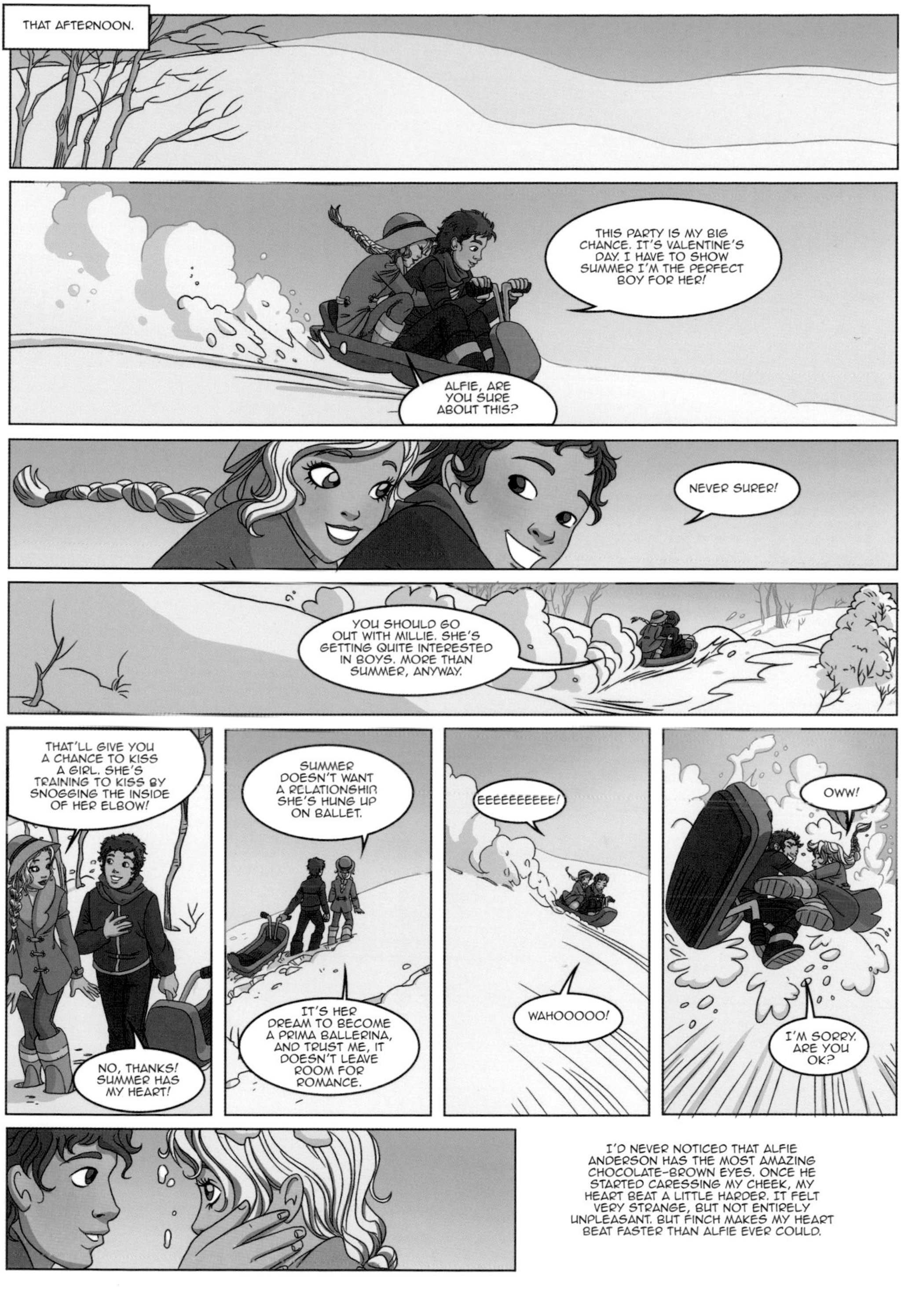
THAT AFTERNOON.
THIS PARTY IS MY BIG CHANCE. IT'S VALENTINE'S DAY. I HAVE TO SHOW SUMMER I'M THE PERFECT BOY FOR HER!
ALFIE, ARE YOU SURE ABOUT THIS?
NEVER SURER!
YOU SHOULD GO OUT WITH MILLIE. SHE'S GETTING QUITE INTERESTED IN BOYS. MORE THAN SUMMER, ANYWAY.
THAT'LL GIVE YOU A CHANCE TO KISS A GIRL. SHE'S TRAINING TO KISS BY SNOGGING THE INSIDE OF HER ELBOW!
NO, THANKS! SUMMER HAS MY HEART!
SUMMER DOESN'T WANT A RELATIONSHIP. SHE'S HUNG UP ON BALLET.
IT'S HER DREAM TO BECOME A PRIMA BALLERINA, AND TRUST ME, IT DOESN'T LEAVE ROOM FOR ROMANCE.
EEEEEEEEEE!
WAHOOOOO!
OWW!
I'M SORRY. ARE YOU OK?
I'D NEVER NOTICED THAT ALFIE ANDERSON HAS THE MOST AMAZING CHOCOLATE-BROWN EYES. ONCE HE STARTED CARESSING MY CHEEK, MY HEART BEAT A LITTLE HARDER. IT FELT VERY STRANGE, BUT NOT ENTIRELY UNPLEASANT. BUT FINCH MAKES MY HEART BEAT FASTER THAN ALFIE EVER COULD.

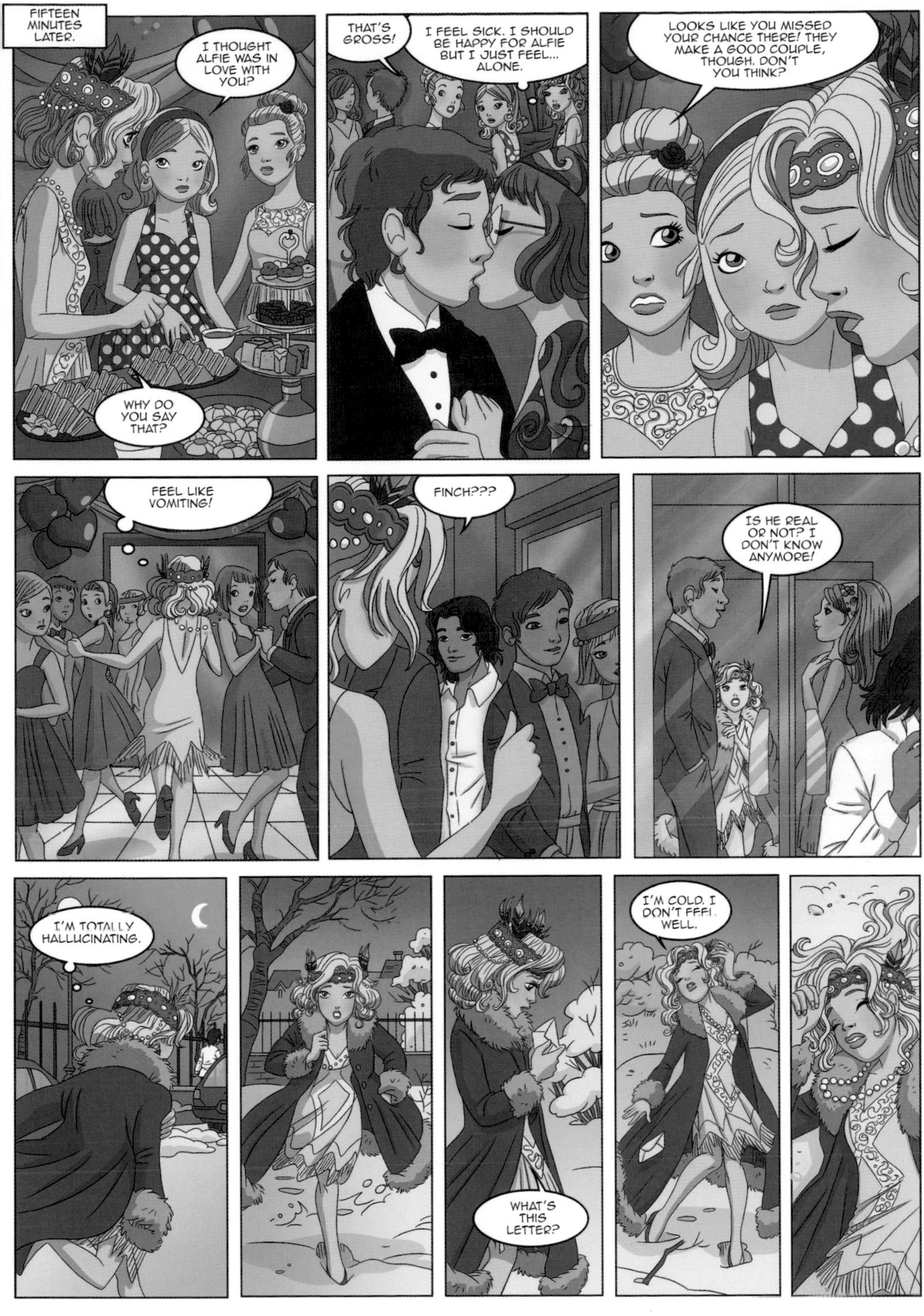
FIFTEEN MINUTES LATER.
I THOUGHT ALFIE WAS IN LOVE WITH YOU?
WHY DO YOU SAY THAT?
THAT'S GROSS!
I FEEL SICK. I SHOULD BE HAPPY FOR ALFIE BUT I JUST FEEL... ALONE.
LOOKS LIKE YOU MISSED YOUR CHANCE THERE! THEY MAKE A GOOD COUPLE, THOUGH. DON'T YOU THINK?
FEEL LIKE VOMITING!
FINCH???
IS HE REAL OR NOT? I DON'T KNOW ANYMORE!
I'M TOTALLY HALLUCINATING.
WHAT'S THIS LETTER?
I'M COLD. I DON'T FEEL WELL.

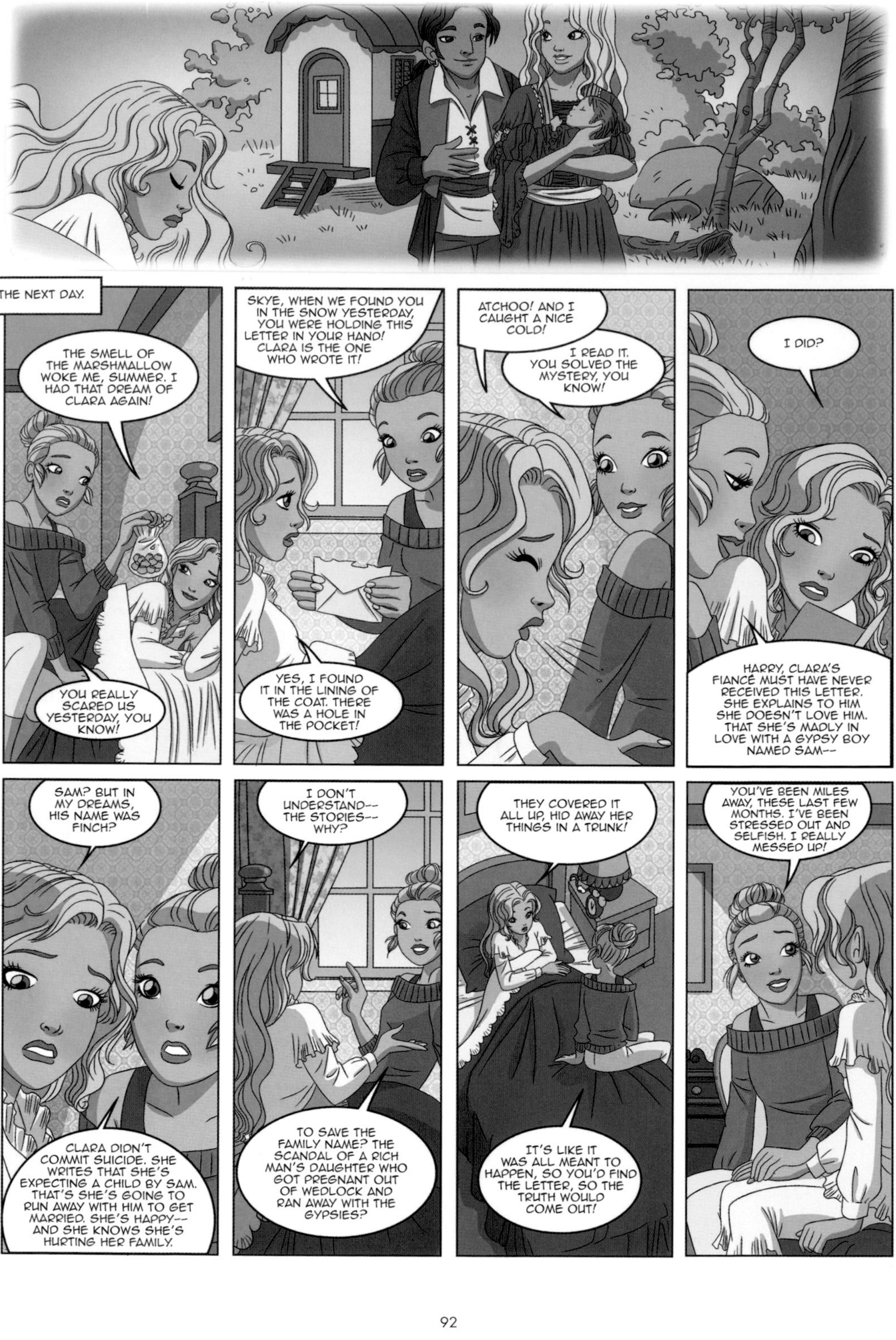

THE NEXT DAY.
THE SMELL OF THE MARSHMALLOW WOKE ME, SUMMER. I HAD THAT DREAM OF CLARA AGAIN!
YOU REALLY SCARED US YESTERDAY, YOU KNOW!
SKYE, WHEN WE FOUND YOU IN THE SNOW YESTERDAY, YOU WERE HOLDING THIS LETTER IN YOUR HAND! CLARA IS THE ONE WHO WROTE IT!
YES, I FOUND IT IN THE LINING OF THE COAT. THERE WAS A HOLE IN THE POCKET!
ATCHOO! AND I CAUGHT A NICE COLD!
I READ IT. YOU SOLVED THE MYSTERY, YOU KNOW!
I DID?
HARRY, CLARA'S FIANCÉ MUST HAVE NEVER RECEIVED THIS LETTER. SHE EXPLAINS TO HIM SHE DOESN'T LOVE HIM. THAT SHE'S MADLY IN LOVE WITH A GYPSY BOY NAMED SAM--
SAM? BUT IN MY DREAMS, HIS NAME WAS FINCH?
CLARA DIDN'T COMMIT SUICIDE. SHE WRITES THAT SHE'S EXPECTING A CHILD BY SAM. THAT'S SHE'S GOING TO RUN AWAY WITH HIM TO GET MARRIED. SHE'S HAPPY-- AND SHE KNOWS SHE'S HURTING HER FAMILY.
I DON'T UNDERSTAND-- THE STORIES-- WHY?
TO SAVE THE FAMILY NAME? THE SCANDAL OF A RICH MAN'S DAUGHTER WHO GOT PREGNANT OUT OF WEDLOCK AND RAN AWAY WITH THE GYPSIES?
THEY COVERED IT ALL UP, HID AWAY HER THINGS IN A TRUNK!
IT'S LIKE IT WAS ALL MEANT TO HAPPEN, SO YOU'D FIND THE LETTER, SO THE TRUTH WOULD COME OUT!
YOU'VE BEEN MILES AWAY, THESE LAST FEW MONTHS. I'VE BEEN STRESSED OUT AND SELFISH. I REALLY MESSED UP!

THE END OF PART 2 "THE GYPSY GHOST"

Welcome to

I am definitely obsessed with all things romance. It's fun, it's dramatic, and it's all about love. I think love is pretty amazing, don't you? When your heart beats faster at the sound of someone else's voice or the way they smile, you just feel more alive. And terrified! Or how about when just being around that special someone makes you feel like you're flying? Like you could do anything? Falling in love is one of the most incredible feelings, ever.

Of course, love is also complicated and painful sometimes. They don't call them "crushes" for nothing!

Yet, when I'm feeling kind of meh or sad, the first thing I want to do is read a romance. Maybe it's because everyone falls in love, has heartbreak and heartache. Maybe it's because there's really nothing like your first kiss. Whatever the reason, when I want to feel better, I pick up a romance and settle in. Usually with tea and chocolate, if I'm being totally honest.

Which brings us to Charmz, a new line of graphic novels just for you! With stories from all over the world, Charmz wants to celebrate love. Whether we're hanging out in Somerset, UK, the wilds of France, speeding through space, or waking up in a cemetery, love finds our characters and digs right in.

Whether you're in the mood for a (literally!) sweet tale about sisters, chocolate, and forbidden love, or exploring the mysterious darkness of Assumption Cemetery where vampires and swamp boys romance stitched girls, you'll find a lot to relate to.

My favorite kinds of romance are epic, sweeping, and probably just a little bit hilarious. As seriously as I take love, if you don't laugh a little at the things we'll do for it, well, you'll end up actually lovesick. Which is definitely something the girls in our books have to deal with from time to time. Not to mention fashion faux pas, weird chocolate recipes, ghosts, zombie sheep, and puzzles through time and space!

I've read a lot of romances and I definitely have my favorites. I think the one I would take on a desert island would have to be *Pride and Prejudice* by Jane Austen. I know, it's old, but it's so witty, and funny, and real. It's been adapted so many times but it always feels fresh and relevant. Anyone could be those characters. Me. You.

Aside from editing this line of graphic novels, I'm also writing one: STITCHED. This spooky little cemetery book with vampires, werewolves, swamp boys and stitched girls is very dear to me. It's the book I've always wanted to write, with spectacularly weird creatures, spooky adventures, and lots and lots of awkward, splendid, romance. Crimson Volania Mulch is my favorite kind of girl; complicated, smart, curious, kind…but a little bit preoccupied with her own problems. And way too judgmental. No one is perfect! And if I woke up only knowing my name in a strange place, I might be a little self-involved, too. I mean, just who is that pretty boy she meets on her first night "alive," and where is her mother? What does a badger/hedgehog actually eat? Do werewolves like cupcakes?

What I want Charmz to be for you is like the book equivalent of a hot chocolate; sweet, maybe a little dark sometimes, comforting, and made just for you. You can curl up with our tales, settle in, and enjoy falling in love with our characters just like they fall in love with each other.

Remember: stories matter, love is powerful, and there's nothing like a love story to make you feel alive.

–Mariah McCourt

Please write to me any time about Charmz! mariah@papercutz.com

I would love hear from you.

STAY IN TOUCH!

EMAIL:	charmz@papercutz
WEB:	www.papercutz.com
TWITTER:	@papercutzgn
FACEBOOK:	PAPERCUTZGRAPHICNOVELS
REGULAR MAIL:	Charmz, 160 Broadway, Suite 700, East Wing, New York, NY 10038

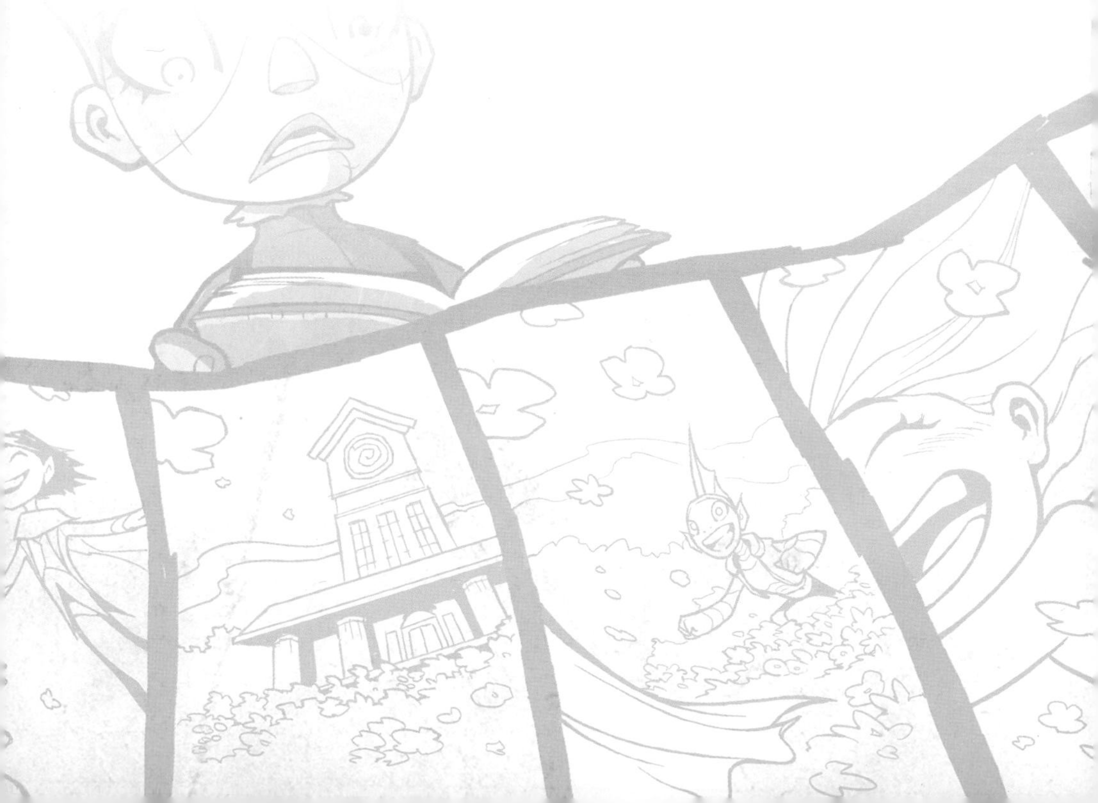